MEL BAY PRES

BANJO PICKING
A COMPLETE METHOD

BY PETER W. PARDEE

CD Contents

m-music   v-vocal commentary

1. Introduction-m/v
2. Tuning-v/m
3. Notation-v
4. Beginning Exercises 1)-m
5. Beginning Exercises 2)-m
6. Beginning Exercises 3)-m
7. The Major Scale-v
8. The Major Scale-m
9. The Major Scale-Filled-v
10. The Major Scale-Filled-m
11. Exercise A-v
12. Exercise A-m
13. Double Shuffle fwd-v
14. Double Shuffle fwd-m
15. Double Shuffle bkwd-v
16. Double Shuffle bkwd-m
17. Reveille I-v
18. Reveille I-m
19. Reveille II-v
20. Reveille II-m
21. Careless Love I-m
22. Careless Love II-m
23. Down In the Valley I-v
24. Down In the Valley I in G-m
25. Down In the Valley I in C-v
26. Down In the Valley I in C-m
27. Down In the Valley I in F-v
28. Down In the Valley I in F-m
29. Down In the Valley II in G-m
30. Down In the Valley II in C-m
31. Down In the Valley II in F-m
32. John Hardy I-m
33. John Hardy II-m
34. Typical Bluegrass Rolls-v
35. Typical Bluegrass Rolls-m
36. By the Beautiful Sea-v
37. By the Beautiful Sea-m
38. Welcome to Eda-v
39. Minuet in G-v
40. Minuet in G-m
41. Reveille III-m
42. The Hussler Minor Jig-m
43. Allegro-v
44. Allegro A-m
45. Allegro B-m
46. Cupid's Arrow-v
47. Cupid's Arrow-m
48. Blackberry Blossom-m
49. Swipesy Cake Walk-v
50. Swipesy Cake Walk A-m
51. Swipesy Cake Walk B-m
52. Swipesy Cake Walk C-m
53. Swipesy Cake Walk D-m
54. Swipesy Cake Walk E-m
55. Swipesy Cake Walk F-m
56. Swipesy Cake Walk G-m
57. Swipesy Cake Walk H-m
58. Double-v
59. Double-m
60. Dominant Study #10-m
61. Thanks to Engineer-v

Pete Pardee-banjo
Eda Pardee-keyboard
Pat Cloud-banjo on Dominant Study #10
Recordists: Pete Grant
        Ron Brandon (Minuet, Allegro,
          Cupid's Arrow)

1 2 3 4 5 6 7 8 9 0

Visit us on the Web at www.melbay.com — E-mail us at email@melbay.com

ACKNOWLEDGEMENTS

First, I give my sincere thanks to my wife, Eda, the love of my life, for her patient advice and bolstering of my resolution.

To the Lord Jesus Christ, and His Word: "**1 John 5:20** And we know that the Son of God is come, and hath given us an understanding, that we may know him that is true, and we are in him that is true, *even* in his Son Jesus Christ. This is the true God, and eternal life." and "**John 1:14** And the Word was made flesh, and dwelt among us, (and we beheld his glory, the glory as of the only begotten of the Father,) full of grace and truth."

To my uncle, Arthur B. Pardee, PhD, for his generous assistance which made this project possible and who has been a great source of inspiration and encouragement all my life.

To Bill Keith, for his phenomenal insights, talents, advice and friendship.

To the late Dave Guard for sharing his system of notation, combining music and tablature.

To Christopher Parkening for his God given musicianship, the clear elegant simplicity of his instruction books (especially Volume 2 with David Brandon as co-author), and for his generosity and advice. Thanks also to Sharon DeVol, Christopher's secretary, for her efficient professionalism and enablement, and to both for the Christian testimony active in their lives.

To David Gottlieb who resurrected the *Nightingale®* music notation program. *Nightingale® 4.5.2, Nightingale® X v. 5.1.0, Claris Works® 5.0, Apple Works® 6.2.9, Adobe Illustrator® 8.0.1* and *10.0.3* and *Power Rip 2000™ 6.0 Professional* were used in the production of this book on an Apple® G3 computer.

To Chuck Waldman and Frank Ford for the photos so well rendered, and for the use of Chuck's Schall banjo.

To the banjo players from many genres, living or deceased, who have been an inspiration. Most significantly, James Bland, Parke Hunter, Joe Morley, Horace Weston, A. A. Farland, Vess Ossman, Fred Bacon, Alex Magee, Fred Van Eps, Frank Bradbury, William J. Ball, Eli and Madeleine Kaufman, Andy King, Peter LaBau, Charles McNeil, Emile Grimshaw, Bud Wachter, Harry Reser, John Cali, Perry Bechtel, Freddie Morgan, Gene Sheldon, Don Van Palta, Charlie Tagawa, Hal Goodwin, Henry Lea, Frank King, Snuffy Jenkins, Bobby Thompson, Allen Shelton, Bill Emerson, Don Stover, Don Reno, Don Wayne Reno, Larry McNeely, Bob Letterly, Alan Munde, Eddie Adcock, Bob Black, Ben Eldridge, Doug Dillard, Bobby Hicks, John Hartford, Dave Guard, Billy Faier, Eric Van Der Wyk, Pete Seeger, Peggy Seeger, Mike Seeger, Tom Paley, Tommy Jarrell, Walt Koken, Reed Martin, Art Rosenbaum, Taj Mahal, Eric Weissberg, Pat Cloud, Dennis Caplinger, Jerry Garcia, Pete Grant, Marty Cutler, Earl Scruggs, Peter Wernick, Tony Trischka, Bela Fleck, Doug Mattocks, Michael Easterling, Dave Guarente, Curtis Wright, Richard Jones-Bamman, David Guptill, Hiro Arita, Lauck Benson, Bill Evans, Bruce Stockwell, Lynwood Lunsford, Sammy Shelor, John Bullard, Jim Carr, Tom Lucas, Bob Bowden, Carl Pagter, and Chuck Waldman. Doubtless I'll regret I've excluded some names, and know I'll hear and meet more players.

Sincere thanks to Bill Bay, Sheri Schleusner, Julie Price and Rachel Cooper at Mel Bay Publications for their assistance in bringing *Banjo Picking—A Complete Method* to the market. To Janet Davis for her recommendation to Bill Bay which set the project in motion, and to all those who have so graciously written endorsements for the book.

Peter Pardee

DEDICATION

In loving memory, to
my late parents-in-law, Henry B. Christopher and
Alma E. Christopher, who helped us get
our first Apple® computer.

Contents

PREFACE TO THE SECOND EDITION

In re-writing this book, my goal has been to appeal to all fingerstyle banjoists. I've provided information to enable a player to develop solid timing and explore rhythms through lots of exercises and musical examples including bluegrass, classic fingerstyle[1], contemporary classical banjo[2] and jazz. Once some of the basics of this book are learned, any other music the player may want to play, such as folk or Celtic tunes, can be adapted to the banjo.

After twenty years, this second edition includes all the information from the first edition, improved graphics, clearer language, plus some significant additions:

- Arrangements of public domain tunes (and two tunes used by permission) demonstrating the use of rolls in several genres
- Playing rolls on one string
- An introduction to reading music, tablature, and a special universal banjo notation
- Photographs
- Projects in **Appendix C** for more development of tunes and skills

The book is now divided into sections. The **Beginner's Section** starts at square one. There is then the **Intermediate** section for players with some experience. The **Advanced** section has more difficult material, and then the **Extreme** section has extremely challenging pieces and exercises. Lots of examples are in each section, which will enable you to develop your skills with rolls in songs. The **Appendices (A, B, and C)** have supplementary information to help you improve your playing and understanding of music and notation.

Banjo Picking can also be used by teachers for students to learn at their level.

Above all, enjoy these exercises and tunes. Use the exercises to warm up, and as a means to improve your playing skills and timing. Progress with patience, *making sure* you can play examples well before moving on to more difficult exercises and tunes later in the book.

Go to it! Nothing can take the place of regular well-planned practice and *playing* the banjo. I hope you'll find this book a great help in improving your timing, tone control and musicianship.

Pete Pardee
Mi Wuk Village, California
August 28, 2002

---

[1] "Classic fingerstyle" is the term the American Banjo Fraternity uses for the urban banjo music which flourished mostly between about 1860 until 1915, and also found followers in England. The Fraternity remains the custodian and primary vehicle for the preservation of this music. In recent years, they've done a lot of research and playing of the stroke style (also their term) referring to the minstrel banjo styles of playing which are identical to drop thumb clawhammer playing.
[2] This is *my* term for transcriptions I and other musicians have done, usually for steel strung resonator banjos and using "true rolls" whenever possible to enable notes to sustain and "sing" as I believe the composer intended

INTRODUCTION

While teaching the banjo, I put together a series of exercises to teach my students to have perfect control of any picking finger. That means for the thumb and two fingers to play with equal strength and skill, with *any* finger able to accent *any* note at *any* time. The first inspiration for these studies came from Bill Keith's exercise on page 60 of the book he co-authored, *Earl Scruggs and the Five String Banjo*[3]. I expanded upon those six four-note patterns.[4] They total 24, because one digit is always followed by a different finger. Only 18 of them use all three fingers.

What is a roll? For the purposes of this book, a "roll" is *four* notes played by a sequence of picking hand fingers (usually the thumb, index and middle fingers) on the five strings of the banjo. A "**true roll**" (there are 320) is one in which no string is played twice in a row (consecutively) and one in which no picking fingers play twice in a row (there are 24 sequences of two and three fingers). There *are* familiar eight note roll patterns (and those will be covered), but all 81,920 won't be dealt with!

The right hand (read "picking hand" or "left hand" if you're left-handed) is the source of most of the timing and tone of your playing. This book presents a unique method to develop and improve the accuracy and versatility of the picking hand. Here's a summary of what's in the book:

The Beginner's Section

The **first** section gives you tips for setting up and tuning your banjo. After that are the most important basic exercises for acquiring right-hand *control*, *timing*, and *articulation*, and learning precise control for *any* order of picking fingers. That order, because three fingers play four notes, is according to where any finger repeats, or plays again. There are some easy arrangements to get you started with familiar tunes.

The Intermediate Section

The **second** section looks more closely at hand positioning and finger movement. The illustrations present the choices for a player in hand positioning and striking strings, with or without picks. Furthermore, the spacing of the notes is explored, that is, being "in the groove", "playing with drive", or "bounce" by looking at just how notes are emphasized and the rhythms that are produced.

All 320 (5x4x4x4) possible "true rolls", that is, rolls in which no string is played twice consecutively are given. The subdivisions are:

I   any two strings
II   any three strings
III any four strings

These are arranged to be played a few at a time, or from beginning to end. The right-hand fingerings given work well for the sequences given, but there are other options, too. Besides being good exercises, these patterns offer choices which will ultimately improve your playing in bluegrass as well as presenting a multitude of arpeggiation and melodic possibilities for jazz or jazzy lines (consider line **I** of "any four strings"—that is, strings 1, 2, 3 and 4; with any four note chord, these represent every possible ordering of the four chord tones), and tackling the intricacies and demands of classical music and other types of music.

The examples in this section are more difficult because they require more skills (manual dexterity) and will require more practice.

After the examples, you'll find all the rhythmic possibilities resulting from leaving one or more notes out of four-note sequences and triplets. Accents on any one or more notes are also explored. These might be thought of as rolls with interruptions. Practice these to improve your understanding and feel of

---

[3] *Earl Scruggs and the Five String Banjo* New York: Peer International Corporation, 1968.
[4] These are distinct sequences which include the three digits: the thumb, index and middle fingers.

rhythms and to add to your creative bag of tricks. Some of these rhythms occur commonly in lots of music. Halving, quartering, doubling, tripling or quadrupling their value and considering the many combinations will prepare you for nearly any rhythmic eventuality in sheet music or in your own improvising. Consider that an eighth note pause (in $\frac{2}{2}$) or a sixteenth note gap (in $\frac{2}{4}$) allows *any* finger to pick again after that pause. This gives you time to think and get around many difficulties. Practice these to improve your understanding and feel of rhythms and to add to your creative store of information.

The Advanced Section

Examples in the **third** section are more difficult to master than in the intermediate section and involve more complex rhythms, too. There are Bach, jazz and classic fingerstyle examples. Then, *all* the possibilities (permutations) of playing four notes on five strings ($5^4 = 625$) are given, and they accommodate numerous right-hand fingerings. It should serve more as a reference than an exercise. They will increase the versatility of your picking hand, though.

The Extreme Section

Material in the **fourth** section includes several contexts in which rolls are used, from Ragtime, Bach, and jazz. Also there are exercises I've found very useful for eliminating pick noise and really finding a balance between all picking fingers by playing rolls on one string, and incorporating the challenge of combining the 18 rolls using all three picking fingers with the 24 sequences of fretting hand fingers. This helps achieve the coordination and absolute independence of both hands.

The Appendices

Appendix A gives more information on reading music notation for the banjo with some music theory.

Appendix B has accompanying parts for some music in the main text, the alternate classic fingerstyle notation for *The Hussler Minor Jig*, and the piano part to *Cupid's Arrow*.

In **Appendix C** I've included several projects to help you develop your playing skills and arrange your own music.

What You'll Need

Besides your banjo, the following tools and accessories are needed:

1) A **metronome**—to learn to keep a steady beat and play each note with the right "spacing".

2) An **electronic tuner** and/or **tuning fork** (**A 440** or **G 392**)—for the ear training to learn to tune your banjo. See the "Ear training" suggestions throughout the book to develop your ear.

Optional suggestions: An experienced **banjo teacher**, and a **tape** or **CD recorder** to record yourself. Though not absolutely necessary, **playing along** with recordings on tape, CD's, MIDI backups or vinyls is another way to learn to play in time, though you should learn to play with good timing *slowly* with the metronome. Then, bit by bit, play faster before you try to play at the speed (or *tempo*) of many recordings.

Because the banjo is often played with other instruments in a band, or other type of group or with an accompanist, finding someone to play with (especially someone who's experienced) will enable you to get "in the groove", that is, to play with exact, steady timing and to get a real "feel" for the music, which is one of the things music is all about.

The Beginner's Section

Four foundations to be established for any musician who plays a stringed instrument are as follows:

1) **Tuning, setting up** and staying in tune.
2) Learning good **timing**, that is, developing a sense of rhythm.
3) Good **tone** (or *timbre*), which is the result of good hand positioning, finger movement and finger placement.
4) How to **read** musical **pitch** and **timing** with the use of standard notation or tablature.

Tuning and Setting Up Your Banjo

First of all, your banjo should be looked at by a knowledgeable player or repair person to make sure that:

1) The **strings** are new and light gauge.[5]
2) The **tuning pegs** are of good quality and adjusted to *keep* the strings in tune.
3) The **head** is tensioned properly.
4) The **bridge** is placed correctly, and is a height allowing for low, light action.
5) The bridge and nut **slots** do not allow the strings to bind.
6) The **neck** is adjusted for a fairly low *action* (height of strings above the neck).

Electronic tuners are readily available in most music stores or from online merchants, but it is better to develop the ear a little at a time so that you'll be able to tune the strings open and recognize that bridge placement is correct to allow for excellent *intonation*, or the "in-tune-ness" of fretted strings.

After making sure the six steps above are done, the first step is to learn to tune the fourth string to "D" below middle **c** from the electronic tuner, pitch pipe, tuning fork, or other instrument. You'll find that:

1) The *fourth* string should turn around the fourth string peg in a counter-clockwise direction in a tight, helical spiral like a compressed spring. After anchoring the string in the peg hole, a minimum of about four turns on the string will "grab" enough on the peg to keep the string from slipping. More turns will be needed for the other strings, as they are of smaller diameter. Turning the peg button clockwise (as you're facing or looking at the back of the banjo peghead or "headstock"), will cause the pitch to go higher, and, as you would expect, turning the button counter-clockwise will cause the pitch to go lower. This is also true for the third string. The second and first strings wrap around their pegs in a

---

[5] This author recommends beginners start with light gauge strings. Heavier strings may be preferred once a player has established his personal tonal and manual preferences.

clockwise direction, so that a counter-clockwise turn of their buttons will cause the pitch of the strings to rise, and, again, drop with a clockwise turn. With the fifth string peg, whether geared or not, turn counter-clockwise to raise the pitch, clockwise to lower the pitch.

 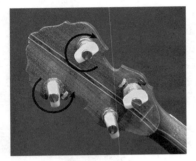

If you're fortunate enough to have Keith® banjo tuners (usually on second and third strings, but available for the first and fourth strings), the two set screws on each tuner housing lock the pitch to one high note, and one lower note of your choice for use in various tunes written or yet to be written for the banjo, and for a quick and accurate change of tuning.

If you have side tuners for your first through fourth strings with strings turned around the peg as mentioned above, the third and fourth strings require a clockwise turn, and the first and second a counter-clockwise turn to raise pitch, and vise-versa for lowering pitch.

2) You *must* listen to the string as it is being tuned to hear the changing pitch. You'll get better at this as your ear is trained from lots of listening.

3) With light gauge strings, and if the string has not been bent so much as to cause it to weaken, you shouldn't have a problem with string breakage.

Never
turn the instrument toward you while tuning!!

Pat Enright, singer and guitarist for the Nashville Bluegrass Band, lost his eye this way. He was tuning a mandolin, fingerboard facing him. The string broke, hitting him in the eye. *Always face the instrument strings away from yourself (or anyone else) while tuning!!*

Ear Training: I use an "A440" tuning fork, which will make the fourth string vibrate because of the *harmonic* at the 7th or 19th fret—but that will be discussed in the Intermediate section.

The G tuning

The common method of tuning by frets to "G" tuning is as follows, even if you have *no* reference, and then you'll be at least "relatively tuned" (the banjo will be in tune with itself):

1) Tune the fourth string to D^6 below middle c^7 or reasonably taut (not too much or too little tension).
2) Fret the fourth string at the fifth fret, **G**, and tune the third string to match.
3) Fret the third string at the fourth fret, **B**, and tune the second string to match.
4) Fret the second string at the third fret, **d**, and tune the first string to match.
5) Fret the first string at the fifth fret, **g**, and tune the fifth string to match.

So, we have the open strings on the banjo tuned:

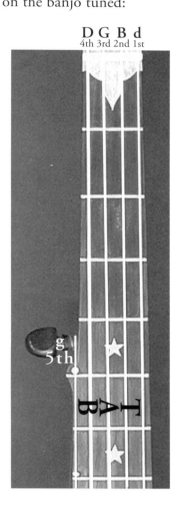

D G B d
4th 3rd 2nd 1st

<u>Ear Training</u> Once the banjo is tuned by the above method, where errors can add up by the time you get to the fifth string, you can learn to hear how both *D*'s (fourth and first strings) and both *G*'s (third and fifth strings) sound together. Then check how the second string, fretted at the third fret (*d*) sounds against the open fourth (*D*) and that there's a *unison* (exact same) pitch with the first string (*d*). The second string should also be checked at the eighth fret (*g*) against the open third string (*G*), and be in unison with the open fifth string (*g*).

---

[6] With middle **c** represented as small case, the lower octave is in capital letters. More is discussed in the appendix.
[7] Middle **c** is so called because of its location near the center of the piano keyboard.

Beginning Notation

Tablature

To begin looking at the notation used here, we'll look first at *tablature*:

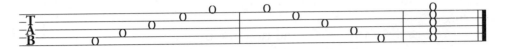 

Turn back to page 13, then turn it 90° counterclockwise to compare to these examples. These lines represent the five banjo strings as you see them when playing. The zeros represent open strings, and the zero is placed resting on the top of the line of the chosen string. First, they're shown played one at a time, then all at once, and are in a stack, which is also known as a *chord*. Then, there's a type of tablature some now prefer, where the tablature straddles the line. I prefer an interrupted line if tablature is going to be written this way:

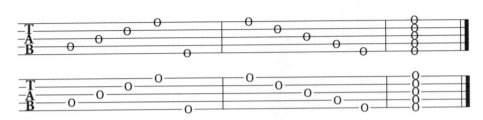 

As you see, stacked notes in a chord are easier to read if the lines are interrupted. This author prefers the former method of having note numbers resting *on* the line.

Music Notation for the Banjo

A combined system of notation especially for the banjo is introduced here for the first time. The five staff lines represent the five strings of the banjo also, strings one through five from top to bottom. O's, are placed in the four spaces between staff lines, and above the top line representing the five open strings of the banjo. Otherwise, the numbers used on the staff lines are *not* fret numbers, but **the four left-hand fingers**, that is:

Index   - 1
Middle - 2
Ring   - 3
Little   - 4

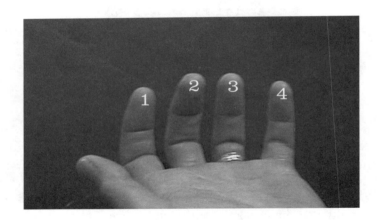

In the beginning, intermediate and advanced sections, most music examples and exercises with fretted strings also have tablature. Most exercises use only open strings, that is: **0**'s. In most exercises, the combined tablature and notes are in half a measure of $\frac{2}{2}$ time, or in $\frac{1}{2}$ time. Below are the five open strings, played from low to high. The fourth string is played first, followed by the third, second and first strings. Then the highest note, the *g* (open fifth string) is played.

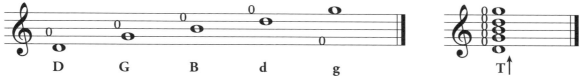

On the right is a chord, the notes are stacked, and can be strummed down with the thumb. These are the open strings of the banjo in *G tuning* in *music and tablature combined*. Notice how the notes, which are whole notes (**o**), balance on the staff. You can see the *D* note (open fourth string), the lowest note, sits just below the bottom line of the staff. Then the highest note, the *g* note (open fifth string), is sitting upon the top line of the staff. The open second string, the *B* note, straddles the middle line, the third line from the top or bottom lines of the staff. The open third string, *G*, straddles the second line from the bottom, while the open first string, *d*, straddles the second line from the top. The music alphabet can be seen in use on the staff lines and spaces as follows:

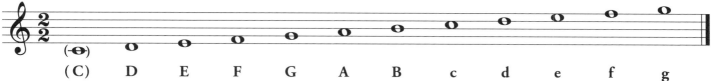

To the right of the tablatures on page 14, the same notes excluding the open fourth string, *D*, show music and tablature combined. "P" means "position number", and the number indicates the fret the index finger is to be placed. "3P" means "third fret", where the index finger is fretting the second string. Translated to tablature:

The right hand fingers used are indicated by: **T** - thumb;   **I** - index;   **M** - middle.

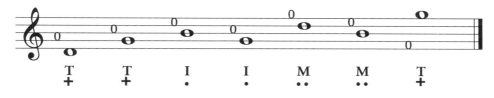

Classic fingerstyle notation uses:

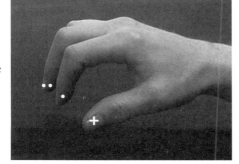

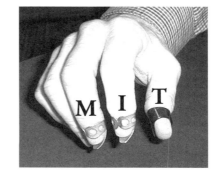

Beginning to Play - Placing the Picking Hand

First, hold out your picking hand (Fig. 1). Then, relax your hand as in Fig. 2 below. Bring your hand over to the area of the strings, at about the middle of the banjo head (Fig. 3).

 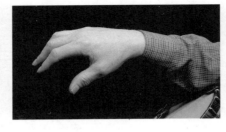 

Fig. 1   *Fig. 2*   *Fig. 3*

Next, curl your fingers a bit more (Fig. 4). Then, bring your elbow a little out from your side, and let your thumb, middle and index fingers raise up above the strings so that your middle finger hovers near and above the first string (Fig. 5). Drop your hand down so that your little *or* ring finger touches the head. The thumb, index and middle fingers should be in alignment, all ready to play at the same distance from the strings (Fig. 6). Later, you may like to try resting *both* the ring and little fingers lightly on the head just below the first string, but for now try at least to rest either the ring or little finger on the head. With the forearm rotated on the armrest as shown below, the thumb, index and middle fingers describe a line nearly parallel to the bridge. The thumb should hover just above the third and fourth strings, slightly more toward the fourth string, but should move near the second or first strings just before playing them. The index finger rests just above the second string so as to reach the third or second string in nearly equal time. If the index is to play the fourth string it should hover nearer the third string just before picking.

Fig. 4   *Fig. 5*   *Fig. 6*

When you get to more advanced exercises where the middle finger is going to play the second third or fourth string, it will rest nearer the second string before it gets ready to pick. It is more difficult to bring the middle finger to inside strings if the thumb plays further from the bridge than the fingers. Of course, experiment with the thumb out further from the bridge, too, and learn to hear the different variety of tone .

At first, learn to pick with bare thumb and fingers. Pick down with the thumb, and use the down side of the pad (under the left side of the thumbnail near the end of the thumb), to strike the string. The first joint of the thumb should be rigid. Consequently most movement will be at the *wrist* joint with some movement at the second joint. In the resting position, the fingers and thumb should be able to touch the head or a table or desktop all at once—then they should all be lined up evenly with the plane of the strings. The index finger moves from its resting position toward the wrist almost as if scratching. The middle finger's movement is similar. Some players bend the thumb at the first joint, but this causes problems with the thumbpick striking a string at the proper angle. Some will prefer always playing without picks—the classic fingerstylists especially, who use nylon strings as well.

16

Once you are playing with ease and fairly fast with no picks, try a set of two metal fingerpicks and a plastic thumbpick. The illustrations below show some range of bending the picks, and the length of the bill of the thumbpick to match fingerpick length.

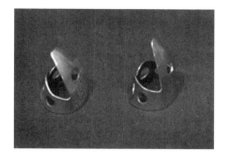

Fig. 7

Fig. 8

Fig. 9

Make sure that the fingerpicks hit the strings either down the middle of the of the picks or to the thumb side. The thumbpick should make a sound as much like a fingerpick as possible when it plays a string. It can be adjusted (twisted by placing in hot water to soften it[8]) to strike the string flatly:

Fig. 10

Fig. 11

The picks will feel awkward at first. After a while though, they will feel quite natural and wear in such a way that the fingerpicks will get shiny where they've been striking the strings. The thumbpick may need some smoothing, which can be done using corrugated cardboard (cardboard box material).

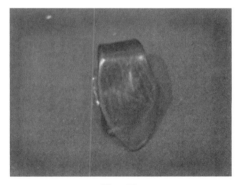

Fig. 12

---

[8]You can pour boiling water in a Pyrex measuring cup and drop the plastic thumbpick in until it softens. Pull it out with tongs, bending and shaping it as desired with your fingers (this may take a few tries) and holding until it sets in the new shape.

Beginning Exercises

1) Set the metronome at M.M. ♩ = 44 or slower to start. With this, pick with the thumb, index, and then the middle finger, playing each note *exactly* with the click of the metronome.[5]

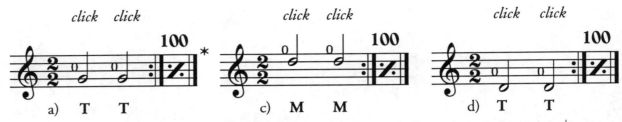

b) **I   I**   With these and the exercises following, *gradually* increase to M.M. ♩ = 100.

Now, use the thumb, middle and index fingers playing on other strings:

2) Below, play the "and" counts and notes between every click of the metronome. These are full measures, in ²⁄₂, of quarter notes. M. M. ♩ = 63 or slower.

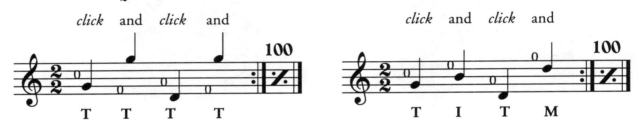

3) With this next roll, play each thumb note with the click of the metronome at M.M. ♩ = 60.[6] Because the thumb is playing at the first and third beats, it can continue in a steady rhythm. This is sometimes referred to as a "square" roll—it's balanced, or symmetrical. Gradually increase a notch at a time to M.M. ♩ = 120:

＊This sign (:‖)means to repeat everything before it. This (✗) and the number above it tells you how many times to repeat it (**100**).

---

[5]M.M. stands for Maelzel's Metronome, not "metronome marking."
[6]This will seem painfully slow, but your patience will result in a good, solid sense of rhythm as you slowly increase the speed or *tempo* using the metronome.

In the next examples another element in counting comes into play. On the left side, the fourth eighth note is left out of the above examples. The right side exercise leaves out the second eighth note. Counting out the left side example, we can recite "*click* and *click*, *click* and *click*", or "*one* and *two* [the and is silent], one and *two* [and]". The right side second note is silent, so the counting will be "*click* [and] *click* and, *click* [and] *click* and, or, *one two* and, *one two* and. These are interrupted rolls. The rhythms will take a while to get used to. Play these starting at M.M. ♩ = 60, and work up to M.M. ♩ = 120. Below the staff is a "grid" of eighth notes with a diamond shaped notehead, *not* to be played, but as a guide for rhythm and counting:

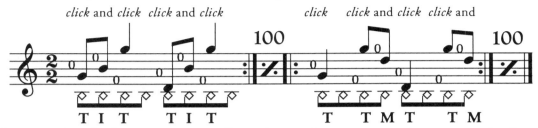

Now, putting the last two patterns from the previous page together, *accent* the first and fifth note, playing with more force with the thumb. This step shows the beginning of carrying a melody by the thumb, bringing out that melody by playing a little harder (with more volume). Later, you'll learn how to use the index and middle fingers with more volume. M.M. ♩ = 60 – 120.

Next, go back to M.M. ♩ = 60, now clicking once every *four* notes. This is the same tempo, (the fingers are playing just as fast), but the clicks are only half as often:

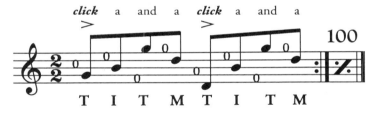

Gradually increase the metronome settings until you're up to about 100. Slow back down if you're not keeping time with the metronome. The last two exercises are full measures of 8 eighth notes.

A Look at the Major Scale

This example, in both tablature and music notation, is a **G** major scale, the familiar *do-re-mi-fa-sol-la-ti-do*. Play evenly and in time with the metronome, M.M. ♩ = 84-100:

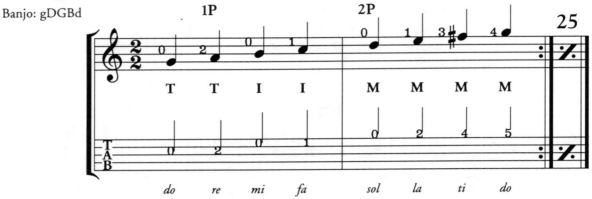

Now play the major scale with "fill in" notes. This is getting closer to the way rolls are used to convey a melody, with some extra notes filling in to make the notes flow faster and include part of the harmony that goes along with those notes of the major scale. This also uses the *six basic finger combinations*: **TI, TM, IM, IT, MT,** and **MI.** M.M. ♩ = 60–120.

When you're able to play the above exercise smoothly and up to at least M. M. ♩ = 104, move on to **Exercise A** on the following page.

Exercise A uses all the four note possibilities with two and three fingers, and should be played slowly and fairly loud. Work at having equal volume and tone on all notes on all strings—use a metronome, starting at M.M. ♩ = 88. Next, accent only the *first* of every four notes, then the *first* and **third of every four notes.** Then, gradually move up the metronome to M.M. ♩ = 132 or higher.

Exercise A

Banjo: gDGBd

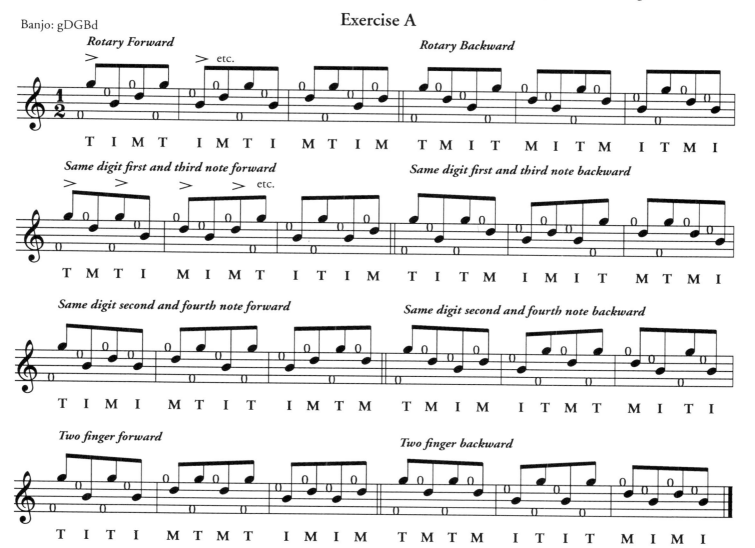

Exercise A shows the 24 combinations listed above according to where the repeated finger occurs. The *rotary* rolls start and end on the same finger. Three go "forward" and three go "backward". The same digit picks on the first and third note in the next category, again, three go forward and three go backward, but the "forwards" start as a backward roll and end as a forward rotary roll, and conversely, the backward rolls in this category start as a forward roll and end up as does a backward roll. In the next category, the same digit plays the second and fourth notes, three go forward and three go backward. The last category is rolls using two fingers only, and one digit plays the first and third notes, while another plays the second and fourth notes.

Exercise A is confined to strings 1, 2, and 5, and also the middle finger plays only the first string, the index only the second, and thumb only the fifth string. Try playing it steadily and slowly enough to get through it without a mistake. For this and any of the exercises following, use your metronome to help you attain a smooth and ultra-precise picking hand.

21

Forward and backward rolls automatically produce a shuffle or *syncopation* very much like the "double shuffle" heard in fiddle tunes like *Orange Blossom Special*. Below are examples of each:

Try these at M.M. ♩ = 76—144. Then go back to M.M. 𝅗𝅥 = 72–152.

Now, using the roll patterns from **Exercise A**, play these rolls with the accents. There are two ways to do this: One is to play **Exercise A** all the way through with one accent at a time. The second way, if you're feeling ambitious, is to continue to play all rolls with the fourteen accents changing with each roll. That would mean starting with the **IMTM** roll the second time through. Playing it through 18 times will cover all rolls with all accents. To get all "*g*" notes, fret the first string at the fifth fret, and the second string at the eighth fret.*

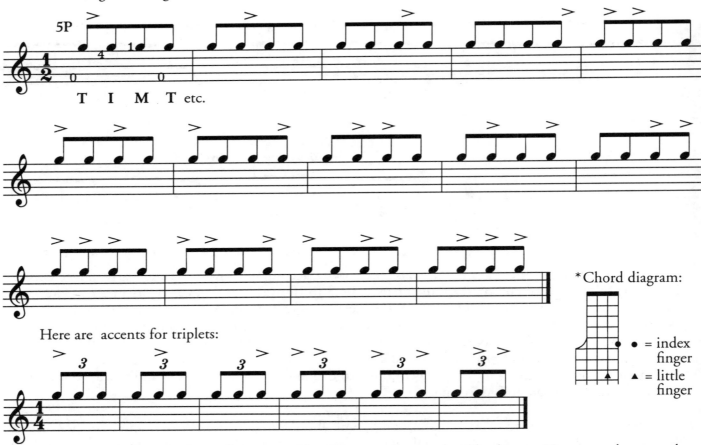

*Chord diagram:

• = index finger

▲ = little finger

Twelve two or three picking finger combinations can be used with these. Here are those twelve combinations: **TIT, TIM, TMI, TMT, IMI, IMT, ITI, ITM, MIT, MIM, MTI, MTM.**

Triplets are explained in **Appendix A**, page 100.

22

Beginning Tunes

Reveille: The "G" tuning is an open "**G chord**", and bugle calls can be played on those open string notes. *Reveille* is in music, first the plain melody with the grid of eighth notes for comparison, and next with some rolls. The accents in the version with rolls show where the melody notes are.

I've used *Reveille*, but on your own, try *Taps* or other bugle calls to get familiar with those tunes and the sound of the G chord notes.

Careless Love: This is the melody of *Careless Love* as sung on an early recording by the father of bluegrass music, Bill Monroe. It is first shown with the melody only, again with the grid of eighth notes for a reference. It is important to learn the *melody*, and then later fill in the gaps with eighth notes. *Careless Love II* is arranged with rolls, which are part of the harmony. The notes above the words (lyrics) are the notes to bring out, the melody. Those "fill in" notes provide the rhythmic drive which makes bluegrass banjo exciting, effective, and interesting to hear.

Play this melody several times, with the metronome at ♩ = 80—120. You're picking out the basic melody, and with the grid you can count to fit those melody notes to the song as it's sung. You'll be singing with the banjo instead of your voice.

Down in the Valley: This is a tune in $\frac{3}{4}$, sometimes called "Waltz Time" and is written in three keys, **G**, **C**, and **F**. In these, only six eighth notes per measure are needed, at least in the beginning stages, for a tune in waltz time. As before, the melody, then with rolls, where all stay pretty close to the timing and melody of the first examples. The melody, must be brought out. It stays very close to the timing of the rhythm of the melodies given above.

The version in **F** is played much further up the neck. More left hand work is required to use this melody with rolls on the following pages. Instead of using the first string **B** natural note at the ninth fret, uses a note one fret lower, the **B♭** note played at the eighth fret of the first string. This is the only scale tone which is different than the key of **C**. The examples in the key of **G** use an *F♯* note. The key of **F** has one flat, and the key of **G** has one sharp. The key of **C** has no sharps or flats. See **Appendix A** to learn more about keys and scales, and how they are created.

John Hardy: As with *Careless Love*, the melody first, followed by the melody with rolls, which are "helper notes". This is a wonderful folk tune, and should be part of any bluegrass banjoist's repertoire.

A few other things to pay attention to in all the arrangements:
1) The **right-hand fingering**: Play the melody with the fingers indicated below the staff.
2) The **position marks**: "1P" means that the left-hand index finger is positioned at the first fret, even though it doesn't fret a string. The position remains in effect until changed, or until a series of open strings are played.
3) The **ties** in measures 8,12 and 16 of *Reveille* and 3, 7,8, 11-12 and 15-16 of *Careless Love*. The third string is played open, then the fourth string is fretted at the second fret, and that note is *not* played again, but keeps ringing into the next quarter note.
4) The **repeat mark** :‖ , which tells you to go back to the beginning and play it once more.
5) **First** and **second endings**. Play **Reveille I** through measure 16, the first ending.⌐1. Then the repeat mark sends you back to measure 1, the beginning of the repeat, ‖: . Play through measure 15, then skip to the second ending, ⌐2. ⌐ and play it.

REVEILLE I

Banjo: gDGBd

Traditional
Arrangements: P.W. Pardee

REVEILLE II

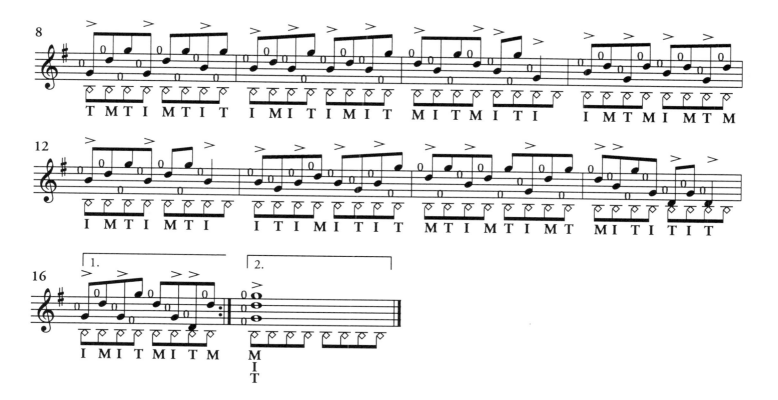

CARELESS LOVE I

Banjo: gDGBd

Traditional
As Sung by Bill Monroe
Arr. for Banjo: P. W. Pardee

Love - oh love oh care - less love.

oh love oh care - less love.

oh love, how can it be, you

love some - one and don't love me.

†These notes should be played at the fourth string *fourth* fret and the third string *second* fret, as indicated by the position mark above the staff. Otherwise, the fingering and tablature would be exactly the same.

Before Playing *Careless Love II* :

You'll be making the **D** and **C** chords, and at other times fretting only parts of chords in this arrangement. There are two extra left-hand skills to develop:

1) In measure 15, the left-hand middle finger (**2**) frets the fourth string at the second fret and then, staying fretted, the left arm moves to the right until **2** is at the fifth fret. It is known as a **slide**, because there has been a slide from fret 2 to fret 5 on the fourth string.

2) In measure 16, the left-hand middle finger (**2** again) firmly and quickly frets the fourth string at the E note (2nd fret). This is known as a **hammer-on**.

The additional new items are the **triplets** used with the slide and hammer on. These are three notes in the space of two. Go to page 42 to see an explanation and to see how they should be counted.

Banjo: gDGBd

Traditional
Arrangement: P. W. Pardee

Measures 7, 14, 15 in tablature:

DOWN IN THE VALLEY I

Banjo: gDGBd

Traditional
Arrangement: P. W. Pardee

Notice the small dotted half notes above the tablature stems. These show how long to let a note ring. Notes longer than a quarter or dotted quarter note are difficult to express in tablature, and, truthfully, aren't often seen in bluegrass banjo tablatures. When they are, the same indication (the small half note with or without a dot) is usually seen. Whole notes were used in *Careless Love*, page 26. In the intermediate and occasionally in the advanced section, those notations are used with tablature only. Keep in mind that the music notation should be referred to for precise duration of notes (how long the notes ring). After this, only a few tablatures in this book have all these helper notes. **Appendix A** has more information about note values and timing.

DOWN IN THE VALLEY II

The ties in measures 5, 6, 11 and 12 for the examples in G and C are there to show that those notes are melody notes. They are picked again in measures 5 and 6 to reinforce the melody, and need to be picked much louder than other notes in measures 11 and 12.

JOHN HARDY I

Banjo: gDGBd

Traditional
Arr. - P. W. Pardee

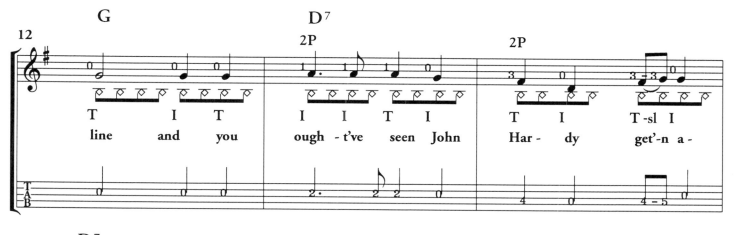

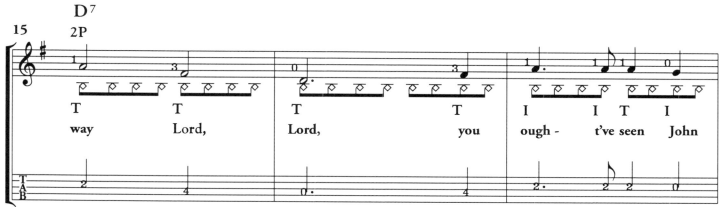

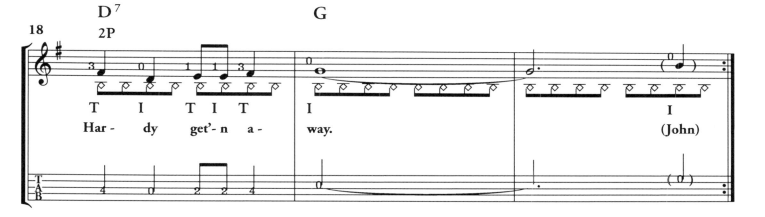

JOHN HARDY II

Banjo: gDGBd

Traditional
Arrangement for banjo - P. W. Pardee

The Intermediate Section

Positioning the Right (Picking) Hand

If you've been playing the banjo a while you've probably found a picking-hand position that works for you to produce the tone you like at any volume. If you've just started to play, consider experimenting with the examples below and find what best suits your anatomy and enables you, with the greatest comfort, to produce the tone and volume you want.

For stability, start with either the ring finger or the little finger resting lightly on the banjo head. Later, learn to rest both the ring and little fingers on the head—but this is a very individual matter, so experiment.

Because everyone is made differently, there are nearly as many right (or picking) hand positions as there are banjo players. In this book, we're dealing with three digits—the thumb, index and middle fingers (though some players also employ the ring finger instead of or in addition to the middle finger). Most players rest the ring and little fingers on the banjo head for greater stability, though others rest only either one or none at all. Doug Dillard rests only his little finger while tucking his ring finger up into his palm. Billy Faier, at times, uses all five fingers.

Three attitudes need to be considered in establishing a picking hand position that will work best for you:

    1) Rotation around the circumference of the head and the side to side bend of the wrist which results in:

        Fig. 13   *Fig.14*   *Fig. 15*

Some banjoists extend the thumb so that it picks further from the bridge than the picking fingers. Others, desiring a more even tone from all digits, align the fingers and thumb so that they're each nearly an equal distance from the bridge.

    2) Forearm angle in relation to the head, and therefore where forearm is on armrest (closer to wrist or elbow).

        Fig. 16   *Fig.17*   *Fig. 18*

Because of the forearm positioning, the arch of the wrist and bend of the fingers varies from a very flat position in which the most bending and movement is at the second knuckle of the fingers to a position in which the wrist is arched, the palm is much further from the strings, and consequently the fingers bend and move mostly at the third knuckle. (Figures 16, 17 and 18)

   3) Rotation of wrist (*radius and ulna - thenar* and *hypothenar eminences*). The thumb side and little finger side of the palm can be rotated to the thumb side (*thenar* - Fig. 19), little finger side *hypothenar* - Fig. 20) or balanced, with both the same distance from the head (Fig. 21).

| *Fig. 19* | *Fig. 20* | *Fig. 21* |

For the necessary power needed to produce solid tone and adequate volume, the wrist should be slightly arched. That enables the fingers to move mostly at the *third* knuckle, including slight movement both at the first and second knuckle, just "giving" a little rather than tense and rigid. Remember also that it is the *downward* (perpendicular to the head) rather than side to side (parallel to the head) movement of the strings that produces the greatest volume and power.

   The fingers and thumb should move in short but powerful strokes. From their resting position, the fingers and thumb make short, elliptical strokes in striking through the string and returning to the rest position. Moving the fingers or thumb in strokes that are too far ranging will hinder speed and efficiency. The only muscles contracting should be the ones that you would use in a "scratching" motion and then *releasing* or *relaxing*, **not** the muscles used in opening your hand, because the muscles on the inside of the forearm would be working *against* the muscles on the back of your forearm and can cause strain and fatigue.

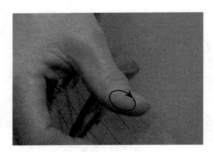 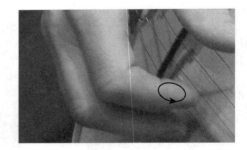

Fig. 22   *Fig. 23*

Following are some often used bluegrass rolls. Pay attention to the accents:

More on Thumbpicks and Fingerpicks

There *are* bare-fingered players (the classic fingerstylists, who, almost without exception, play on nylon or gut strings, play with the bare fingers exclusively), but two metal fingerpicks and a plastic thumbpick are the most common combination. Fingerpick shaping varies from absolutely straight and flat to curled around the ends of the fingers and cupped.

Fingerpicks are worn from flat across the pads of the fingers or are turned with the picking surface toward the thumb side of the fingers. In any case, picks should be shaped to act like your natural picking position without picks, and should be shaped and bent laterally to strike the strings across the middle or thumb side of the pick face. As the picks wear, they should get most shiny either at the center or the thumb side of the pick face. Also, it is generally agreed that the picks should not "bite" too deeply into the strings: 1/16 inch (ideal to remove pick noise), but to no more than to 3/16 inch.

Plastic thumbpicks can be obtained in a variety of sizes and thicknesses. The bill of the pick can be shaped and shortened by rapid movement over cardboard (the corrugated brown cardboard box material) to be blunt or narrow. After that, immersing the pick briefly in very hot water will make it pliable to be shaped to fit just right and to twist the bill to strike the strings flatly for minimal pick noise and the tone production you desire. For those who have smaller thumbs, use toenail clippers (the kind which look like pliers) or wire cutters to shorten the curved "strap" part of the thumbpick and bend it to fit after softening it in hot water. There are many types of thumbpicks available, including metal and picks made with other substances, so you may want to shop for some and experiment.

All three picks can be worn very near the first knuckle, or nearly at the end of the fingers and thumb. There are now many styles of picks to choose from, and some attach *below* the first knuckle.

This author prefers a heavy gauge plastic thumbpick with the bill shortened to produce a comfortable balance with heavy gauge fingerpicks, which are placed well onto the fingers and curved up around the ends of the fingertips. They should be cupped slightly, and twisted laterally toward the thumb. In the resting position, all rest at the same level and that enables equal "bite" on the strings with both picking fingers and thumb.

Remember that the fingers can pick anywhere from just next to the bridge all the way to where the fingerboard joins the banjo head. (Beyond that, there's a risk of striking the frets and fingerboard, but there is a softer tone all the way to the 12th fret, then it sharpens as you go toward the nut). There are a multitude of tonal nuances available between these extremes, even though perhaps 80% of your playing will be done at the location somewhere around 1 1/2 to 2 inches from the bridge where the tone is most clear and loud. But use these tonal choices to the best advantage as your taste dictates.

In bluegrass or jazz, the basic beat or pulse in alla breve, or "cut" time $\frac{2}{2}$ or in $\frac{2}{4}$, is the *half* measure—the half note in $\frac{2}{2}$ or the quarter note in $\frac{2}{4}$. The banjo will usually fill the half measure with four notes (four eighth notes in $\frac{2}{2}$, or four sixteenth notes in $\frac{2}{4}$). In this book we will be concerned with patterns of *four* note rolls as well as the accents and other rhythms that can be used in the half measure. A *full* measure has *two* basic beats or pulses (*ones* or *booms*), and eight eighth notes, or eight sixteenth notes:

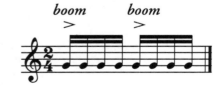

The Basic Building Blocks of Rolls

There are only six elementary right hand movements in three finger banjo—the building blocks of rolls, as we saw in the beginner's section.

1) thumb followed by index - **TI**   4) index followed by thumb - **IT**
2) thumb followed by middle - **TM**   5) middle followed by thumb - **MT**
3) index followed by middle - **IM**   6) middle followed by index - **MI**

Without repeating a digit twice consecutively, there are only 24 (3x2x2x2 or $3x2^3$) four note roll combinations. 18 of them use all three picking fingers. The two finger rolls are the six basic building blocks repeated one after another, and are in italics:

TITI	*ITIT*	MTIT
TITM	ITIM	MTIM
TIMT	ITMT	*MTMT*
TIMI	ITMI	MTMI
TMTI	IMTI	MITI
TMTM	IMTM	MITM
TMIT	IMIT	MIMT
TMIM	*IMIM*	*MIMI*

A measure full (eight notes) has 384 (3x2x2x2x2x2x2x2 or $3x2^7$) possible combinations.

Timing

In bluegrass and jazz, eighth notes bounce along in a rhythm less monotonous than this:

Fig. 26

The actual rhythm is something approximating this:

Fig. 27

Dividing the half measure into 24ths, here's the difference:

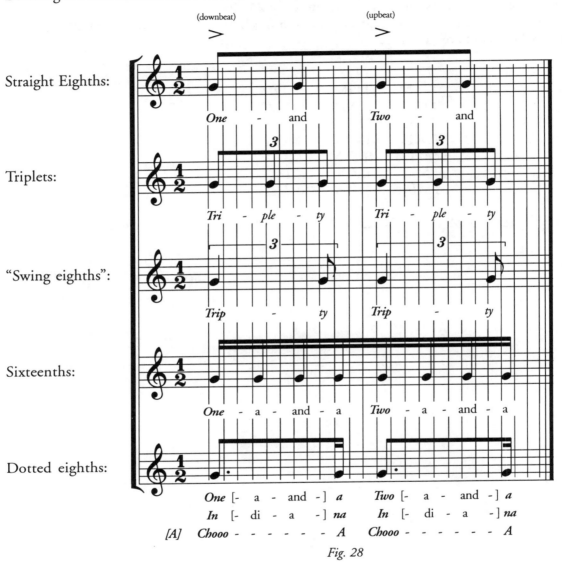

Fig. 28

The sixteenth note after a dotted eighth note is 1/24 of a half-measure later than a swing eighth. The first note of a swing eighth lasts twice the length of the second note. The first note of a dotted eighth lasts three times as long as the second note.

Now try **Exercise A** with the *swing* eighths, remembering the triplet sound, and that the first and third notes of every four note roll last twice as long as the second and fourth notes. Lots of words have that rhythm, but you might try *"trip-ty trip-ty"*. Increase the tempo, one notch at a time again on the metronome, until you come to M.M. ♩ = 208. Then set the metronome to M.M. ♩ = 104 and have the metronome click on *only the first* of four notes. Once you're above the 144 tempo, you're nearly up to speed with the fastest tempos you've heard on recordings.

After becoming familiar with the triplet feel of "swing" eighths, again try some of the accents listed. That means giving just a little more volume to the notes accented (or less on the unaccented ones).

The first ones to use are:

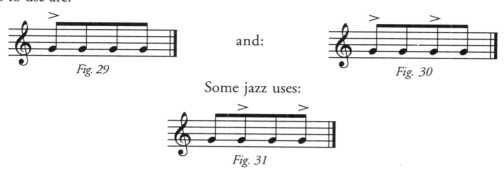

and:

Fig. 29

Fig. 30

Some jazz uses:

Fig. 31

Combine those accents with the swing feel, try **Exercise A** with the metronome and use various volumes. *Crescendo*[11] loudness from minimum to maximum and decrescendo to near silence. You'll begin to capture the smoothness and clarity of articulation which may have been eluding you. It will also be a good test of your finger control, and show you what's needed to avoid pick noise.

The other accents are important as well, so try *all* of them with **Exercise A**. This will enable you to get the emphasis on *any* beat and by *any* finger. An exercise with often-used bluegrass rolls and accents in $\frac{2}{2}$ time is back on page 39. Here's a practice routine:

> 1) Play **Ex. A** fretting first string at fifth fret and second string at the eighth fret with a metronome in swing eighths, gradually increasing metronome speed.
> 2) Play **Ex. A** with as many different accents as you can in swing eighths, crescendo and decrescendo; use the metronome.

The steps in this summary, with the exception of fretting in step 1) can be used with all exercises. The section of any two, three, and four strings can be played in *C tuning* (gCGBd)[12], fretting as in step 1) and additionally at the fourth string seventh fret, producing all "G" notes, the third and fourth strings simply sounding an octave lower than the first, second and fifth.

When playing any of these exercises, you may, of course, make all sorts of chords to relieve the literal monotony of "G" notes or the "G triad" (G major chord) sounds. Next, fretting as the diagram indicates (first string 5th fret, second string 8th fret), **Exercise A** will produce all "g" notes. Strive for equal volume and tone on all notes at first. Cramping of the left (or fretting) hand may result from holding this or any formation over a period of time, so if this happens, give the left hand a rest. **Gradually** increase the metronome setting, but *only as you can maintain complete accuracy*. To go beyond 208, start again at 104 having the metronome click only at the first of every four notes.

---

[11] Gradually increase
[12] Tune the fourth string one whole step lower to "C". Now, the 7th fret of the 4th string should match the 3rd string open, and you should hear an octave (*C* to *c*) at either the 2nd string 1st fret or 3rd string 5th fret.

Each digit (that is, the thumb, index and middle fingers) has a typical conventional function: The *thumb* is the only digit that plays the fifth string; it also plays the fourth string, third string, sometimes the second string, and sometimes, the first string. The *index* finger sometimes plays the fourth string, the third and second string, and sometimes the first string. The *middle* finger plays the first string, sometimes the second string, less often the third string, and, very rarely, the fourth string. With these common guidelines, it's easy to decide which picking finger plays which string. However, these conventions can be broken, and *are* broken later in the book.

Then, try the exercise in swing eighths, finally try it with swing eighths and accents. Next, still with the swing eighths, accent always with the *thumb* first, then the *index* finger, then the *middle* finger. As mentioned in **The Beginner's Section**, this results in the accents producing a sound like the fiddle double-shuffle used in, among many other tunes, "*Orange Blossom Special*".

On the following pages are the 320 true rolls. Again, they are rolls in which no string is played twice in a row, and in which no finger picks twice in a row. Notice the "grips", that is, any two, three, or four strings that are to be played. These are also ways to play *intervals* (two notes at once), or *chords* (three or more notes at once). Learn to play all these "grips" as intervals and chords as well as the rolls exercises.

All of the "**ANY FOUR STRINGS**" sets could be played with use of a fourth picking finger. For sets **I**, **III**, **IV** and **V** though, the thumb can glide and play two strings as effectively as with four fingers. I quote the great Zither banjoist A.D. Cammeyer, from his 1903 book, *The Cultivation of the "Hands" for playing the Zither-Banjo & Banjo*, pages 18 and 19:

> ". . . [I] do not advocate the use of the third [ring] finger, as I consider its aid neither necessary nor desirable.
> The thumb can easily strike both the bass and the third string almost simultaneously with the first [index] and second [middle] fingers picking the second and first strings respectively, so that the effect does not bear the slightest similitude to an arpeggio."[13]

In set **III**, **IV** and **V**, the thumb can also glide across strings four and five. In later examples, these will be looked at. The "*Morley pinch*", named for the great British classic fingerstyle composer and banjoist, Joe Morley, can be used to execute string set **II**. The index finger can glide rapidly upwards across strings two and three. I've devised this symbol for the Morley pinch:

$$\text{mp}$$

The same sequence of right hand fingers as in **Exercise A** can be used for the sets using any three strings, and for the most part with the sets of any four strings, where a few exceptions are indicated by an asterisk (*).

Practice these with the metronome, keeping in mind all the things already mentioned: timing, smoothness, accents, swing eighths, crescendo and decrescendo. Your picking hand, in getting quite a workout, should be increasing in versatility and agility.

---

[13] That is, the sound is of a chord where all notes are played at once rather than one at a time rapidly.

320 TRUE ROLLS

Any Two Strings

Banjo: gDGBd

II, continued

V, continued

† Re-ordered

VIII, continued

ANY FOUR STRINGS

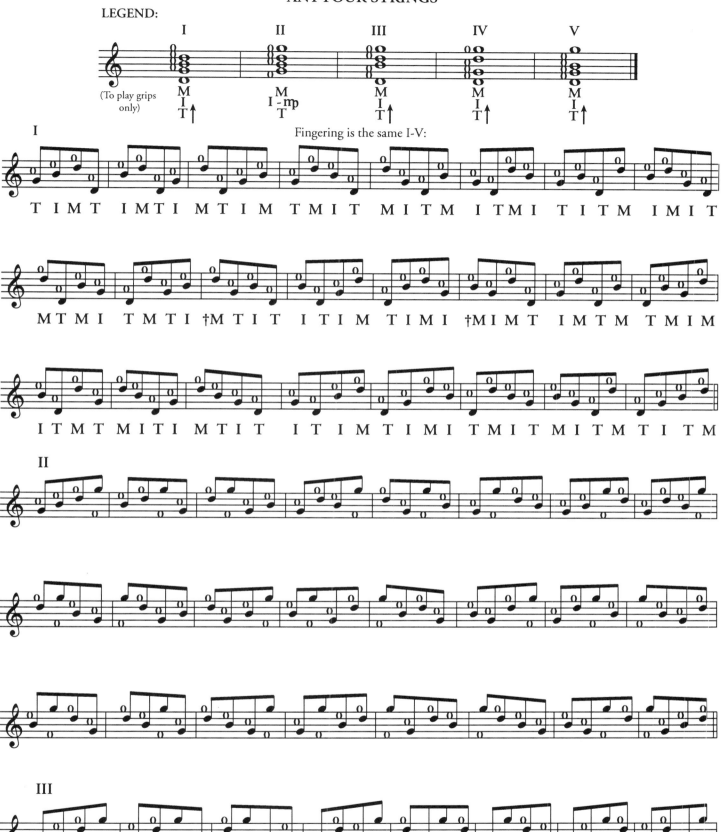

III, continued

More Examples

There are some new tunes following, and there is a more advanced or fancier version of *Reveille*.

I've arranged the old standard *By the Beautiful Sea* with rolls. The rolls are mostly non-stop, designed to help you play a continuous articulated flow of notes. The accented melody is within *another* melody with all the surrounding notes. Those surrounding notes are from the harmony and in some instances are parts of a scale. Play until you have a smooth flow of notes with enough of the swing feel to make it rhythmically exciting—something that would make you or a listener want to tap your feet.

J. S. Bach's *Minuet* from the *Anna Magdalena Notebook*, a collection of easy pieces for keyboard is best played with an accompanying bass. However, it stands on its own as a banjo solo. The banjo part is taken from the *treble clef*, played on keyboard by the right hand. The bass part is the keyboard part, played by the left hand, from the *bass clef*, and is included in **Appendix B**. Let the notes ring, and make the banjo sing*. A Minuet is a graceful dance in a moderate tempo.

Reveille III is now filled in with twice as many notes, and also melody notes aren't right on the usual beats—in other words, the tune is *syncopated*. Lots of different rolls are used to put the melody imbedded in the harmony notes. The ties [⌣] are used to set apart the melody; *the notes are to be played* unless there is no picking finger or fretting finger symbol. There are a lot of interruptions with quarter notes– ♩. Notice that the second ending has a "*G*" note fretted at the 5th fret on the fourth string.

As in earlier examples, pay close attention to the *accents* (they are the melody notes), and give them more volume to bring those melody notes out. Learn to play with swing eighths to give your playing the driving rhythm and "bounce". Play *very slowly* and *gradually* build up more speed.

The Hussler Minor Jig is by the great 19th century banjoist Horace Weston, written in 1881. Weston played in both fingerstyle and stroke style, a general term for frailing or clawhammer technique. In both music and tablature, **Appendix B** also has this arrangement in traditional classic fingerstyle notation. The right hand works differently than in bluegrass music. I've chosen some conventional classic fingerstyle picking hand technique and some not so conventional. *Horace Weston's Celebrated Minor Jig* is another classic fingerstyle piece to investigate.[14]

A jazz sequence is used in **Ex. B**, employing the 24 fingering patterns to execute IIm7–V7 changes in all keys, chord tones only.

Next, all the rhythmic possibilities from a measure of $\frac{1}{2}$ time leaving one or more eighth notes out, and compared with the grid once again, are given. Multiplying or dividing their value in duple or triple times and combining these elements will prepare you for anything you may find in sheet music and for creating your own rhythms.

Right (or picking) hand muting can be accomplished by quickly touching the string or strings played with the pick or finger, being careful not to make pick noise. Left (or fretting) hand muting is done by lifting off a string just fretted with the fretting finger or lightly touching an open string which has just been picked so as to stop its vibration.

*Ear Training: Listen to how the "*A*" note (second fret, third string) reacts with surrounding notes, especially the open first and fourth strings and the *F♯* note on the first string. If you're playing in tune, these surrounding notes will ring so as to give a pleasant, "in tune" sound, and will support the *A* note as all strings vibrating will produce a pleasant, harmonious sound, in measure 29 especially.

---

[14] Contact the American Banjo Fraternity for membership information and a huge library of music.

BY THE BEAUTIFUL SEA

Banjo: gCGBd

Arrangement: P. W. Pardee

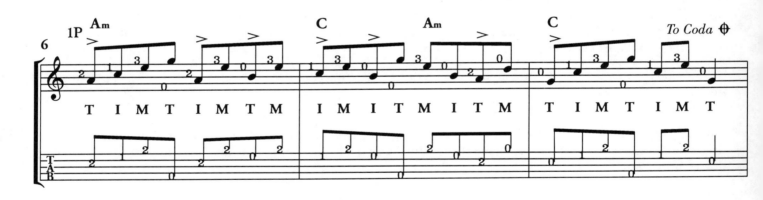

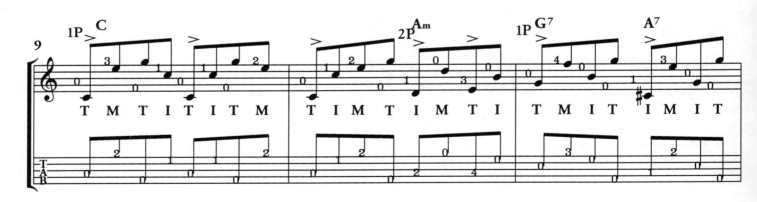

By the Beautiful Sea, concluded

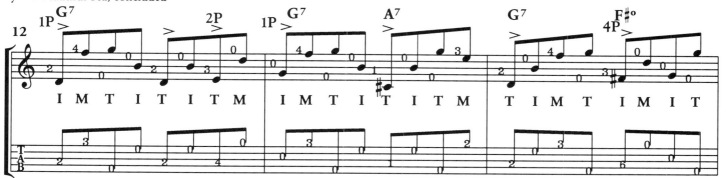

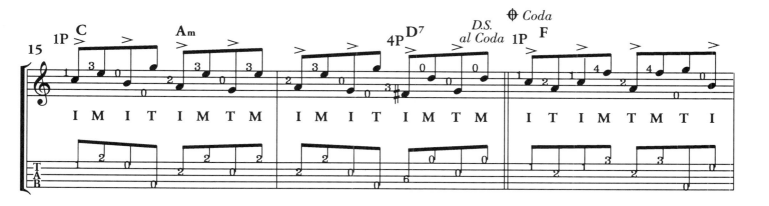

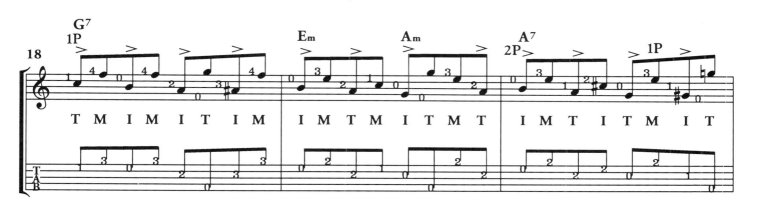

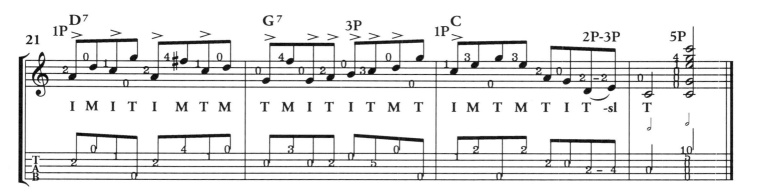

Minuet, continued

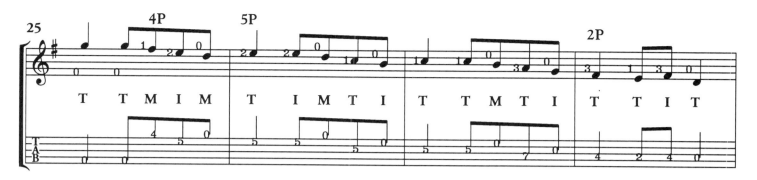

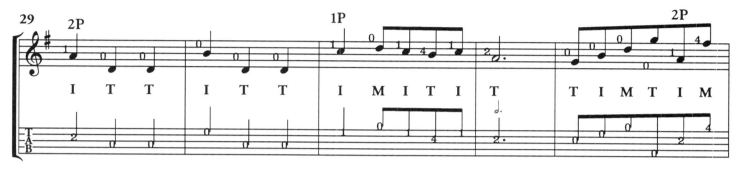

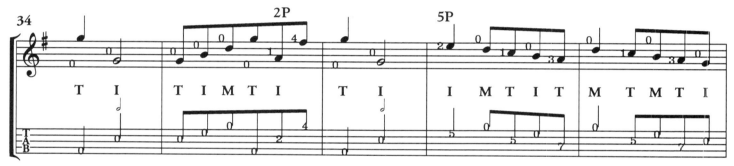

REVEILLE III

Banjo: gDGBd

Arr. - P. W. Pardee

THE HUSSLER MINOR JIG

Horace Weston

This symbol: ⟨ stands for a rapid arpeggio, and so **T**, **I** and **M** are stairstepped, followed by **T**, playing the open fifth string:

*Ear Training: As discussed in the beginner's section, hearing harmonics and octaves is essential in learning to tune your banjo. Just as listening to the octaves on the open 4th and 1st strings (*D* notes), and the open 3rd and 5th strings (*G* notes), a *harmonic* produces a pitch at twice the frequency of the open string note. A harmonic can be made by touching any string over the 12th fret *wire*, and then picking the string. (12 frets higher on the 5th string is at the 17th fret). When a harmonic is played at the 12th fret of a string, the string is divided into two equal parts. Harmonics can be made at 1/3 of a string's length at the 7th or 19th fret. That produces a pitch a *fifth* (five scale notes) higher. On the third string, that would be a *d* note. The same pitch (frequency) is found at the 12th fret of the first string. Harmonics can be made at 1/4 a string's length at the fifth fret (fifth string at the 10th fret). On the fourth string fifth fret, the same *d* harmonic note is produced as on the first and third string mentioned above. I've found that matching even higher harmonics (or partials) covers tuning four of the five strings: 4th string, 1/8 of length between frets 2 and 3; 3rd string 1/6 of length between frets 3 and 4; 1st string 1/4 of length at fret 5; 5th string 1/3 of length at 12th fret all produce the harmonic pitch *d'*. The second string, if fretted at the 5th or 8th fret can either vibrate in *sympathy* (same pitch activated by notes from other strings) or with harmonics at, respectively, the 8th and 15th frets to achieve the *d'* pitch. Slight tuning changes will help these notes become more finely tuned as your ear develops sensitivity to those pitches.

RHYTHMS

Banjo: gDGBd

Exercise B
IIm7-V7 in Fourths

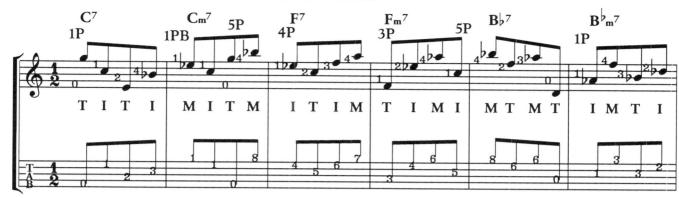

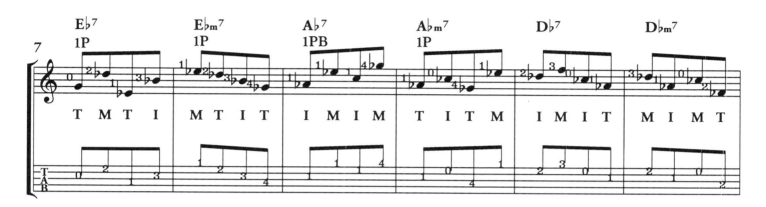

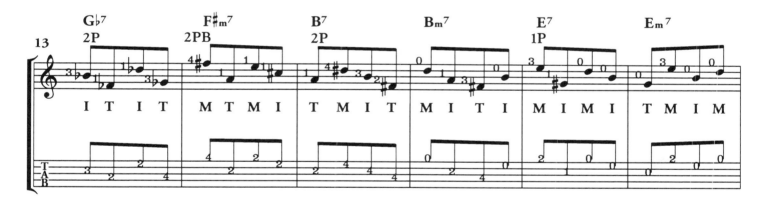

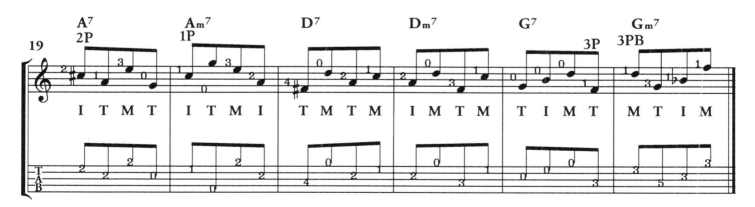

The Advanced Section

First are some more examples. The *Allegro*, by Johann Sebastian Bach, is from the *Prelude, Fugue and Allegro* originally for lute in the key of D major. The author has transposed it to G major. It can be played as a solo piece, or with accompaniment by bass. The bass accompaniment is in **Appendix B**. The first part works out fairly easily, but the second part requires a lot of practice for the fretting hand especially. Practice this very slowly with the metronome after playing and reading through it enough times to anticipate your moves. I've found that "crossover rolls" are indispensable for executing many passages I've discovered in developing my Bach transcriptions. Figure 32 shows the thumb preparing to cross over the index finger, and Figure 33 shows the second string being picked by the thumb. Measure **18** is shown with the **T I T M** picking finger sequence, and here are the photos demonstrating the moves:

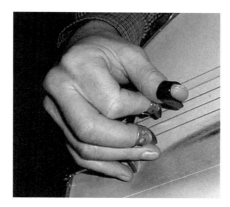

Fig. 32

Fig. 33

Cupid's Arrow is a classic fingerstyle favorite composed by Paul Eno. The transcription was done by the author from a Fred Van Eps recording, and reveals the many innovations and elaborations Van Eps added. As in Horace Weston's *The Hussler Minor Jig*, the picking hand is functioning differently than in the typical bluegrass manner, so has been annotated where felt necessary. In **Appendix B** you'll find *The Hussler Minor Jig* in the standard classic fingerstyle notation.

Beating Around the Bush is an original composition by Bill Keith, well known to banjoists for his fine playing, many contributions to banjo technique, Keith® banjo tuners, his workshops and teaching tapes. A master of the harmonic intricacies of jazz, Bill says this tune came about by its chord progressions first, and then he developed the melody.

I've included two versions of *Blackberry Blossom* starting with a version I adapted from the banjo player Bob Letterly, a clever musician with exceptional creativity and skill. The second time through, more is added by the author to the voices and harmonic complexity of the first version. Many versions are already available of the linear (known to musicologists as *homophonic*) melody, so Bob's version is already a step above that.

Picking hand fingering has not been given, because by now, the player should be able to choose the most appropriate fingerings.

After this, there is no standard tablature notation. With help from **Appendix A**, an understanding of the banjo fingerboard, key signatures, accidentals and the chromatic scale, location of notes and frets should *not* present a problem.

Following the musical selections, all 625 possible four note roll sequences on five strings (5^4 = 625) are given. If these were to be full measures of eight notes, there are 390,625 (5^8) sequences. Picking hand choices for these 625 are too numerous to include, but by now, you are free to explore these.

Ear Training: **As your ear improves, slight tuning adjustments will improve the musicality and intonation when playing in different keys. A composition in G uses different tuning adjustments than one in the key of c (that is, c minor), D or any of the other keys.**

ALLEGRO

From Prelude, Fugue and Allegro
BWV 998

Banjo: gDGBd

J.S. Bach
Transcription: P. W. Pardee

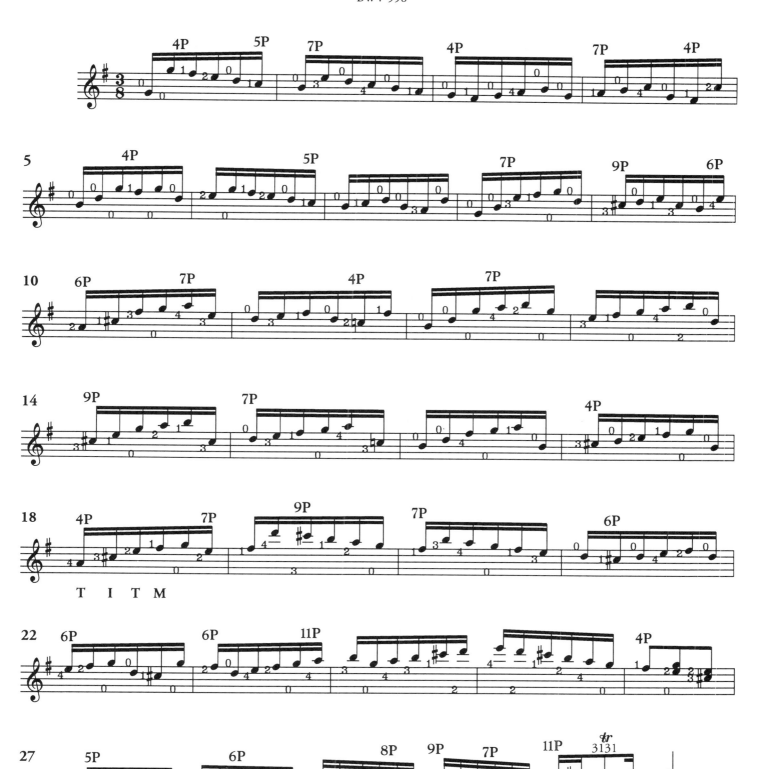

Allegro, continued

Allegro, concluded

CUPID'S ARROW
Grand Polka de Concert

As played by Fred Van Eps
Banjo: gCGBd

Paul Eno
Transcription: P. W. Pardee

[Play intro., A, BB, A. CC, DD, intro., A, BB, A to ⊕, Coda]

Cupid's Arrow, concluded

BEATING AROUND THE BUSH

By Bill Keith

Banjo: gDGBd

Beating Around the Bush, concluded

†This can also be fingered by the thumb - (5).

This is an alternate fingering for measures **5, 6** and **13, 14**.

69

BLACKBERRY BLOSSOM

Banjo: gDGBd

Traditional
Arrangement - Letterly, Pardee

71

Permutation of All Rolls

Banjo: gDGBd

Rolls beginning on first string

Rolls beginning on first string, concluded

Rolls beginning on second string, continued

Rolls beginning on second string, concluded

Rolls beginning on third string

75

Permutation of All Rolls, continued

Rolls beginning on third string, concluded

Fourth string rolls

76

Rolls beginning on fourth string, continued

77

Rolls beginning on fourth string, continued

Rolls beginning on fifth string

Rolls beginning on fifth string, concluded

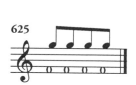

The Extreme Section

You are now at the section which will put your skills to the limit and perhaps open some doors for furthering your abilities and repertoire beyond what you had considered before. By now, the author hopes you are also weaned of standard tablature.

First, the examples. *Swipesy Cakewalk*, by Scott Joplin and Arthur Marshall has the accompanying bass line added to the melody line, adapted for the banjo and transposed from B♭ to C. There are several instances in which you'll need to use the "grips" discussed in the intermediate section on page 44. Listen to a piano version to hear the lilt of ragtime music.

Next, my transcription of the *Double* from J. S. Bach's second Lute Suite in c[15], written in the same key for the banjo. Classical guitarists usually play it in a, though I have seen a transcription in d. This piece has true counterpoint, and works the fretting hand, though it is very important to pay attention to the picking hand sequences as well for smoothness of execution. As in classical guitar, the picking hand thumb is given double duty while the fingers alternate, but there are necessary exceptions.

Last is, through the courtesy of jazz banjoist Pat Cloud, *Dominant Cycle Study #10*, an exercise exploring all key areas, and demanding lots of the fretting hand. This composition is valuable in many ways: exploring key areas, providing source material for improvisational excursions, improving your ear for jazz sounds and supplying the coordinational foundations for demands of playing in the jazz idiom.

The exercises **C** and **D** included here combine all picking hand sequences with all fretting hand finger sequences on one string. First, the fretting hand is given one sequence to play with all 18 three finger picking hand possibilities. Secondly, an exercise is presented that uses all 18 three finger picking hand sequences played with all 24 fretting hand possibilities. When played through eighteen times, all combinations of the two hands will have been explored as you continue the fretting and picking hand sequences. Here are the 24 fretting hand sequences:

1 2 3 4	2 1 3 4	3 1 2 4	4 1 2 3
1 2 4 3	2 1 4 3	3 1 4 2	4 1 3 2
1 3 2 4	2 3 1 4	3 2 1 4	4 2 1 3
1 3 4 2	2 3 4 1	3 2 4 1	4 2 3 1
1 4 3 2†	2 4 1 3	3 4 1 2	4 3 2 1†
1 4 2 3	2 4 3 1	3 4 2 1	4 3 1 2

† These are out of permuted sequence in order that different fingers always follow.

---

[15] Small case is used for minor keys.

SWIPESY CAKE WALK

by Scott Joplin and Arthur Marshall
Arr. P. W. Pardee

Banjo: gCGBd
M. M. ♪ = 72—108

Swipesy Cakewalk, continued

83

Double, continued

Double, concluded

Dominant Cycle Study #10

Banjo: gDGBd
M. M. ♩ = 80—132

by Pat Cloud

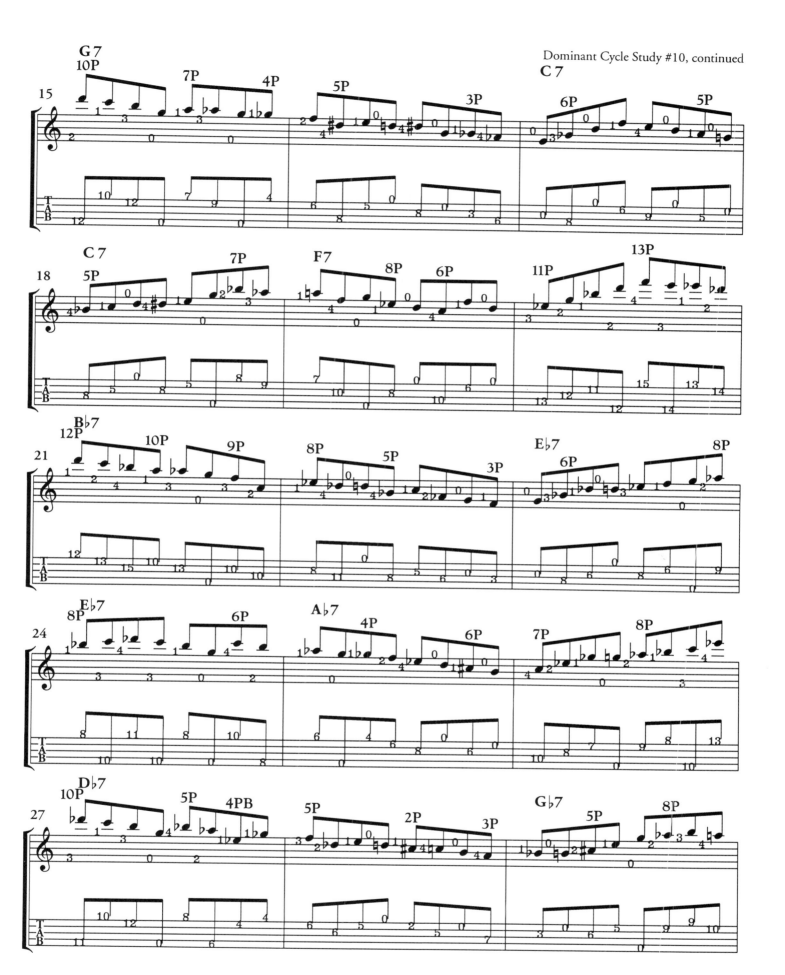

Dominant Cycle Study #10, concluded

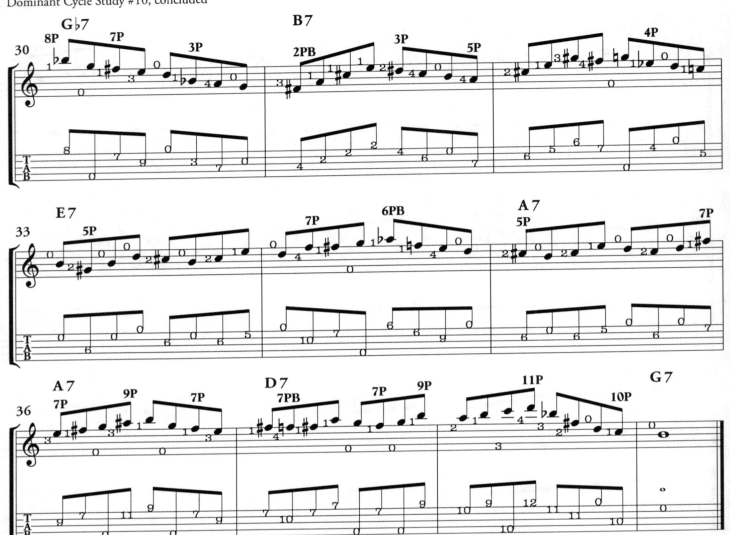

Exercise C

Banjo: gDGBd

All rolls with one fretting hand finger sequence   (3 finger)

Continue with 1 2 4 3, 1 3 2 4, etc.

Exercise D

All rolls with left hand sequence also changing

Continue back to measure 1 with M I M T, etc. Ex. A sequence

Appendix A

More on Reading Music Notation

Music is written in two directions to show how low or high notes are:

Up: ↑
Down: ↓

The passage of time is represented horizontally in one direction—left to right:

⟶

Pitch

Five staff lines are used in music notation:

The *G clef* is used for banjo music:

When placed on the staff lines, the curly, spiral part circles the second line from the bottom of the staff:

That tells us that notes (here shown from a whole note through a sixty fourth note) *on* that second line are "*G*" notes. The open third string of the banjo is a *G* note.

Let's look once again at the open banjo strings on the staff, from low to high tuned strings, and then played all at once as a chord:

How high or low notes are[16] determine where they will be placed on the staff. Notes straddle lines or are placed in spaces on the staff. As notes go higher, the note in the space above *G* is an *A* note, and the musical alphabet starts over. (The space above is *not H*, but we start over at *A*). The English alphabet names the notes using lines and spaces (*B, c, d, e, f*) then to *g*, resting on the top line. From *G*, lines and spaces go down the music alphabet to *F* and *E*, then to *D*, resting just below the bottom line:

---

[16] The open fourth string, *D*, vibrates 146.83 times per second, and the open fifth vibrates at a higher *frequency*, 392 times per second. The highest note which can be fretted on a standard five string banjo is *c"*, 1,046.5 times per second, a yet higher frequency.

Extra *ledger* (sometimes spelled *leger)* lines are added above and below the staff. The banjo is not often pitched below *C*[17]. Anyway, we'll continue down to *A*. The next note below *D* is *C*, straddling the first ledger line, followed by *B* below the first line, then *A* straddling the second ledger line.[18]

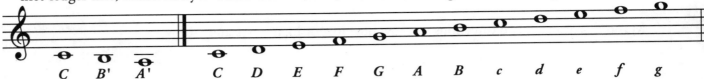

In the extended look at notes above, there are two *C*'s, two *D*'s and two *G*'s, but they're each eight notes (an *octave*) apart. Therefore, capital letters are used for the low octave, and small case letters are used for the higher octave. Within the notes above is the C major scale. The change is made at *"c"* because music was set up this way—*C* is the beginning of the *C major scale* (*do-re-mi-fa-sol-la-ti-do*. On a piano or keyboard, those notes are the *white* keys, known also as *natural* notes.) If we tune the fourth string down to *C*, here is one way to play the C scale on the banjo:

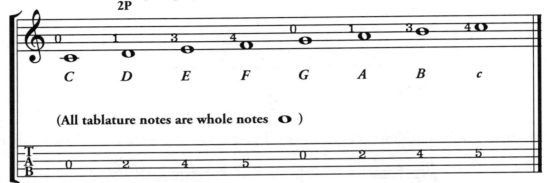

Notice that from the open fourth string *C* the next note, at the second position (**2P**—the second fret) is a *D* note, fretted with the index finger. Next is *E*, again skipping a fret to fret **4**, and fretted with the third or ring finger. The *F* note is fretted on the fourth string, fifth fret by the little finger, but *one* fret above *E*. The next note is *G*, the open third string. On the third string, use the same fingers (**2**, **3**, and **4**) at the same frets (**2**, **4**, and **5**), to make the *A*, *B*, and *c* notes.

A look at the G scale shows that it begins on a *G* note. As you should expect, the *G* is followed by *A*, *B*, and *c*. These are one half of the notes in the scale, known as a *tetrachord*. *G*, *A*, *B*, and *c* are also the last or upper half of the C scale we just looked at. We must use the same number of frets (two, two and one) starting at *d* (the open first string), followed by *e*, *f*♯, and *g* to complete the G scale:

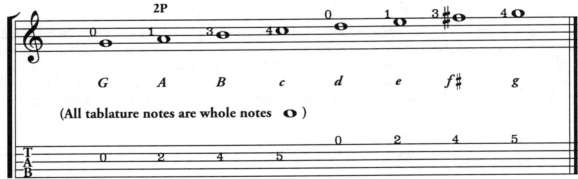

[17] C tuning: gCGBd. Banjo music, like guitar music is written one octave higher than it sounds.
[18] Notes lower than this, for example for minstrel banjos or guitars use up to four ledger lines. For other instruments pitched lower, the bass clef is used. There are even the intermediate tenor and alto clefs for certain instruments.

Tetrachords must be connected by two frets, also known as a *whole step*. The G scale above was completed using the tetrachord: first string open, *d*, (a whole step from *c*). Then, two frets to *e*, and next we must move two frets to *f♯*, *not f*. The *g* note to finish the scale is one half step from *f♯*, just what is needed to complete the scale and tetrachord. For this reason, any tune played in the *key* of G will be written with one sharp as the key signature. (The end of the G scale is also the beginning of the D scale.) The sharp symbol ♯ straddles the *f* line of the music staff. *All F notes are to be played F♯*:

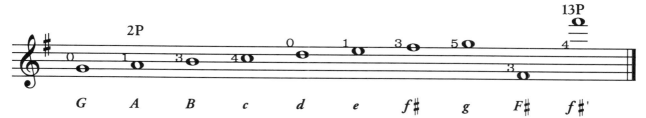

Going back to the key of C, here's the next C scale, which starts where we left off. Now, the C scale is at a higher pitch. The ledger lines and spaces above *g* are *a*, *b* and *c'*:

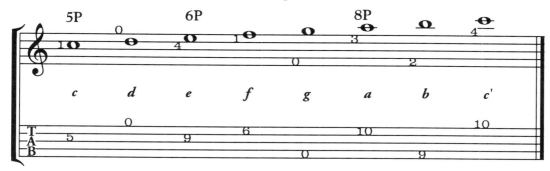

Here's the last C scale, showing first using the five ledger lines up to *c"* and then, below, the symbol *8va* and dotted line are used, where notes are to be played one octave higher than written. Both staffs represent the same pitch. This last octave uses the single quote or apostrophe mark for letters (*c',d',e',f',g',a',b'*) while the highest note (*c"*) has the two marks. There are about 3,000 practical ways of fingering the left-hand notes for the C major scale in this octave, and here are two:

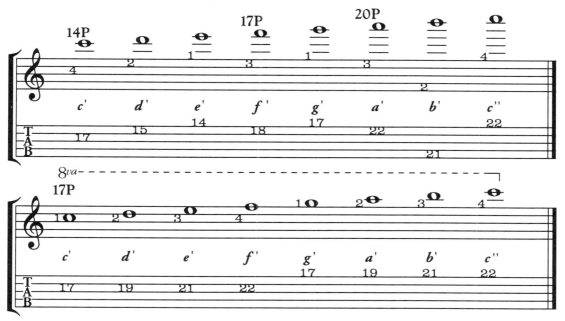

95

The notes on the *in between* frets (that is, on frets 1, 3, 6, 8 and 10 on the fourth string) for the key of C as shown on page 94 are all the sharp and/or flat notes. The same names are used for the notes, and they're on the same lines, but have either a sharp (♯) or flat (♭) sign before them:

Banjo: gCGBd

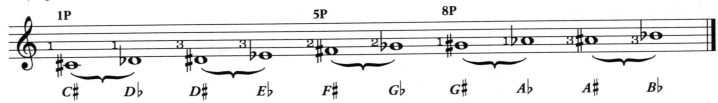

Each fret stops notes a *half step* apart. Notice that one fret can be named with either a sharp or flat. All these sharps and/or flats become necessary to use in the twelve different keys. Playing any string one fret after the next makes the *chromatic* scale. The *natural* symbol (♮) restores a note to its natural pitch. These notes have already been seen on the previous pages as part of the C scale: *D♮ -E♮ -G♮ -A♮* and *B♮*. Played on the fourth, third and second strings, this is a chromatic scale starting at *C*:

The Twelve Major Scales

The tetrachord formula can be used to find the notes of *any* of the twelve major scales, or *keys*, using any note chosen from the chromatic scale. It is best to start with flats for the keys of B♭, E♭, A♭, D♭, and G♭. Except for *F♯*, use the plain alphabet letters for the keys of G, D, A, E and B. A reminder: the key of C major has no sharps or flats. Doing this will help greatly in learning the notes on the banjo fingerboard and where to find them.

Scales for all keys have to be made the same way with tetrachords. The end of the G scale is the beginning of the D scale, and the beginning of the C scale is the end of the F scale. The end of the B♭ scale is the beginning of the F scale. All twelve major scales can be figured out this way, going forward (adding one sharp at a time) *or* backward (adding one flat at a time) with tetrachords. All twelve major key signatures come about by this method.

Once you progress through the keys of G, D, A, E, and B, the key of F♯ has six sharps. Going the other direction, through F, B♭, E♭, A♭ and D♭, the key of G♭ has six flats. It has the same pitches as the key of F♯, but the notes are named differently. These two names for notes are called *enharmonic equivalents*. A step further from F♯ would generate the key of C♯, having seven sharps, while the key of C♭ has seven flats. The key of C♭ is the enharmonic equivalent of the key of B, and the key of C♯ is the enharmonic equivalent of D♭. The circle of fifths diagram illustrates the keys arranged in their cycle on page 97.

THE CIRCLE OF FIFTHS

Here is the circle of fifths with key signatures. Refer back to page 96 (opposite). To make the best use of this diagram, study and work through to the keys of G and then to D, then to F, B♭ and E♭ using the tetrachord method. Within this diagram there is much to be learned about scales, chords and chord progressions.

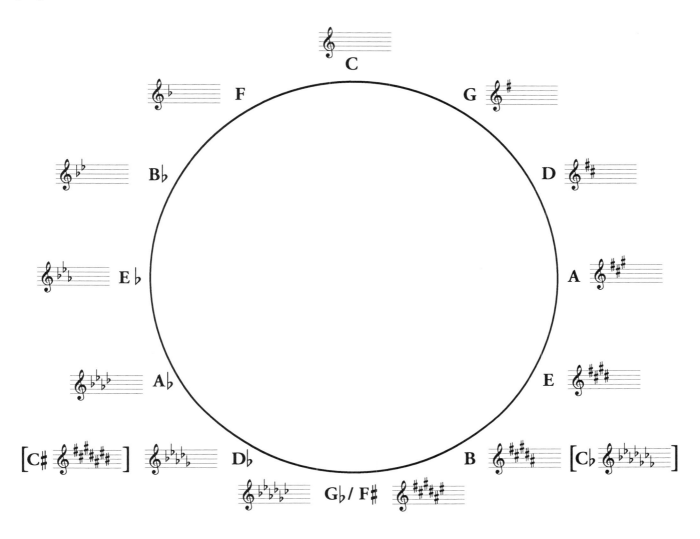

Major Chords and Their Inversions

It is also useful to learn the inversions of major chords. In G tuning, the *root* of the chord *names* the chord, and the root is on the third string (root form), first [and fourth][19] string (first inversion), or second string (second inversion):

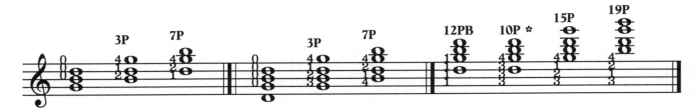

The banjo in G tuning is already tuned with the root on the third string. The notes are *G*, *B*, and *d*, the first, third and fifth notes of the G major scale. The first inversion uses the third and fifth notes on strings three and two, and then the note eight notes higher, *g*, on the first string. To review, those eight scale notes are an *octave*. The second inversion uses the *d* and *g* on strings three and two, then *b*, an octave higher than the second string open, on the first string. All on the twelfth fret, the first, third and fifth notes of the G major scale are an octave higher than the open strings—*g*, *b*, and *d* '. The same chord forms repeat an octave (twelve frets) higher until there aren't any frets left, where the second inversion is at **19P**:

Index •
Middle ○
Ring ◉
Little ▲

Barre or partial barre: ⌒

Chord Tones:
R = Root or first
3 = Third
5 = Fifth

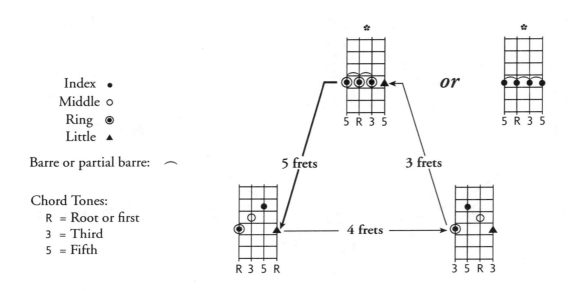

To make any major chord, the first, third and fifth notes of the major scale can be used using the partial barre or full barre chord on strings 3, 2 and 1. The fifth note is *doubled* an octave lower on the fourth string. Numbers below the diagrams show which note of the chord is the first, third or fifth notes of the scale. *__Any__ major chord can be found once you apply the chromatic scale and the inversions shown above.* Notes on the fourth string are always doubled using these inversions. Forms can go as low as open strings or as high as your 22nd fret, or more if you have more frets.

---

[19] Notes on the fourth and first string are the same notes, one octave apart, forming a four note major chord.

The standard for most banjo music in $\frac{2}{2}$ time is eight eighth notes, counted as *one-and-two-and-three-and-four-and*:

Quarter notes are twice as long:

Half notes last twice as long as quarter notes, or ring as long as four eighth notes:

A whole note lasts an entire measure. It is equal to eight eighth notes, four quarter notes, or two half notes:

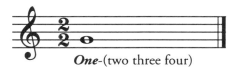

A beam joins flagged notes shorter than a quarter note. Those include eighths, sixteenths, thirty-second notes, and so on:

Two eighths, then two eighths beamed:

Four eighths, then four eighths beamed:

Four sixteenth notes, then four sixteenth notes beamed:

Four thirty-second notes, then four thirty-second notes beamed:

Depending on needs, combinations such as the following show how beams can be grouped or combined in several different ways:

A note which is dotted is equal to the note plus half its value. That means one and a half, equal to three halves. When thought of as three halves, think of the undotted notes as three notes of half the value tied together, which means, once the note is dotted, it's equal to three notes of half the value of the original. Sound complicated? Well, it really isn't. Look at these:

A dotted quarter note equals a quarter note tied to an eighth note, equal to three eighth notes:

A dotted eighth note equals an eighth note tied to a sixteenth note, equal to three sixteenth notes tied:

Notes of larger or smaller duration use the same idea.

Triplets are three notes to be played in the space of two. Count *tri - ple - ty* :

Time Signatures

$\frac{2}{2}$ is the most common time used for most bluegrass tunes, reels, and hornpipes. The fundamental beats are *two half notes* per measure, and that is where the $\frac{2}{2}$ comes from. The bottom number is what kind of note, two indicating that it's a half note. The top number is *how many* of those half notes.

What about $\frac{2}{4}$ time as seen in Pete Seeger's *How to Play the 5-String Banjo*[20] , or in *Earl Scruggs and the 5-String Banjo*, written by Bill Keith and Earl Scruggs? There are still *two* fundamental beats, but they're represented in notes half as long. It then becomes a question of tempo. If M.M. ♩ = 120 in $\frac{2}{2}$, the end result is the same if M.M. ♩ = 120 in $\frac{2}{4}$. The results, when played, are exactly the same, so it's a matter of preference and a question of beaming. $\frac{4}{4}$ has been used erroneously as common practice in much published bluegrass banjo tablature, and should be $\frac{2}{2}$ or $\frac{2}{4}$. $\frac{2}{2}$ and $\frac{2}{4}$ and even $\frac{6}{8}$ (because there are two fundamental beats!) are *duple* times.

$\frac{4}{4}$ is more often seen in jazz, especially after about 1930, in country music, and some slower bluegrass songs, (tunes with the "walking bass"–definitely a feeling of four beats per measure) and in rock music, where there are *four* fundamental beats. $\frac{4}{4}$ is *quadruple* time.

Triple times most commonly are $\frac{3}{4}$ (waltz time) and $\frac{9}{8}$ (many jigs are in $\frac{9}{8}$ or sometimes even $\frac{12}{8}$). As with duple time, the lower number of the time signature indicates the value of the note that gets the basic beat, while the upper number tells how many of notes there are in one measure.

Triplets as seen back on page 42 and 58, are easiest to learn by use of $\frac{1}{2}$ time. Double the number of notes per measure and you'll have $\frac{2}{2}$ time.

---

[21] Seeger, Peter. *How to Play the 5-String Banjo*. Beacon, New York: Published by the author, third edition, revised, 1962.

More On the Banjo Notation

All three major banjo techniques, *fingerstyle*, *stroke* styles (down picking or up picking, which includes clawhammer, frailing and the Pete Seeger "basic strum"), and *plectral* styles (that is, using a flat pick) can be notated using this method.

All five digits of both hands can be put to use. Picking hand fingers are indicated by **T** - thumb, **I** - index, **M** - middle, **R** - ring, and **L** - little finger.

Fretting hand fingers are: 1 - index, 2 - middle, 3 - ring, 4 - little, and 5 - thumb. The author, and most fingerstyle banjoists, use three picking hand fingers and four fretting hand fingers, though a majority of bluegrass banjoists use their thumb to fret the fifth string. O, meaning "open" stands for an open string.

Above the staff, **P** means position number. The number in front tells the fret at which the index finger is positioned. On a standard banjo, that goes from **1P** (the first fret) all the way to **22P** (the twenty-second fret). A *barre*, when a finger "lies down" and frets two or more strings, is displayed as **B**. Barring can be done by any fretting finger, and can cover two to five strings. "**5PB**" means "barre at the fifth fret".

Additional special indications for the picking hand are:

1) The *glide* ↑, preceded by the digit used, such as **T**↑. With the notes above, this symbol is used:

2) The *Morley pinch* **m̄p**, usually executed by the index finger, **I** - **m̄p**

3) Bridge muting, made by resting the left side of the palm below the little finger, the *hypothenar eminence*, using the picking finger letters in outline form: 𝕋, 𝕀, 𝕄 and so on.

4) The *rest stroke*, with a dot after the finger used, for example: **M** ·. This can also be called "pick blocking", and mutes a string after being played.

5) Beyond the scope of this book are *finger and thumb tremolos*, made by oscillating the thumb or fingers both directions rapidly across a string. This symbol is used on the stems of the notes, executed by the finger shown below:
I

There are seven fretting hand techiques which have their own special symbols:

1) The *hammer-on*, also called *slur* by the classic fingerstylists, is played by using a left-hand finger to make a sound by strongly fretting a string. -**h** is the symbol. The sound could be make after playing a string with the picking hand, or (and this takes some power by the fretting hand) by just forcefully fretting a string with any picking hand finger

2) The *slide*, also called *glissando*, which can go **up** in pitch (and more often than not does), or **down** in pitch. -**sl** means "slide". As a note is plucked by the picking hand, the fretting finger moves to another position on the fingerboard.

3) The *lift-off*, -**l**, hardly spoken of, but an effective way of muting a string because a fretting finger eases up on a string, letting it rise above the fret wire but still touching it. For back-up technique, the liftoff "mute" is often heard in bluegrass banjo, in which notes are not fretted all the way but touched by the fretting hand at whatever pitch or chord symbol desired. In this case, an **x** is used above the notehead or tablature number, at the end of the stem.

4) The *pull-off* or *snap* (as the classic fingerstylists call it). A fretted string is played, then the fretting finger plucks the string (usually toward the palm, but sometimes away from the

palm) either leaving it open or remaining fretted by a lower number finger. -p means to pull off.

5) The *choke* or *bend* in which a string is fretted then pushed toward an adjacent string, either toward or away from the palm. Chokes, -ch, sound best when they stretch a string either a whole or half step and **in tune**. An up arrow ↑ means away from the palm, while an down arrow ↓ shows that the choke is to be made toward the palm.

6) *Harmonics* or *partials*, are most often made by a fretting finger touching and then releasing a string at half (twelfth fret), one third (seventh or nineteenth fret), or one quarter (fifth fret) its length. Touch a string over the fret wire, pick it with a picking finger, and let it ring. In *Beating Around the Bush* (page 68) you'll see the hollow diamond note-head and a small H: ◇

7) *Trills* are rapid hammer-ons and pull-offs involving a change in pitch. This kind of ornamentation is seen in classical guitar, baroque music and other genres. The symbol *tr* is found above the notes on the staff and are to be played by the left-hand fingers used to fret the notes. The last measure of *Oh, Susanna* shows the trill fully notated, and the fretting hand fingers used in their entirety above the staff, just below the trill symbol.

8) *Vibrato* is a fretting hand technique most often heard used by cellists, blues guitarists and violinists, and is a rapid or slow (which will depend on how much sustain your banjo has) use of fretting finger(s) moving along the length of a string or strings while firmly fretted, giving a little more sustain and a somewhat warbling sound. Another vibrato technique is to play choke(s) rapidly, altering the pitch only a little. *Vibrato* is written above the staff for vibrato passages, or with a wavy line ∼∼ after the note for a very agressive, pronounced vibrato.

From top to bottom, here's an explanation and rationale for the annotation, those things that help the banjo player/reader:

Chord Symbols - used in the standard manner.

Position Marks - borrowed from classic fingerstyle literature. Classical guitar notation uses Roman numerals, and therefore the notation is "Americanized", though we owe a lot to the British classic fingerstyle aficionados for their contributions, most particularly the "**C Notation**".

The Music Staff - standard in every respect except for the placement of fretting hand finger annotation. The numbers are placed on the lines which also represent the strings of the banjo rather than near the note-heads. They are still on a vertical plane slightly left of the note-heads. Therefore, the notation is combined with tablature, used in banjo notation for more than a half century. Beaming is always above or below the staff to reveal the fingering notation, keeping it clear. Spacing is sometimes altered to accomodate the fingering annotation. All other standard and dynamic annotation can of course be utilized with standard music notation. Music notation is the worldwide standard, and the finger numbers are borrowed from piano, guitar and other instruments. Their placement shows which string is to be played without the need for an additional annotation symbol.

Picking-Hand Fingering - has been borrowed from the standard banjo notation and tablature in use for many years for bluegrass and folk banjo music. T, I, M, and sometimes R and L is the Anglicized banjo version of the classical guitar Spanish *p, i, m,* and *a*. The +,.,.. and ... used by classic fingerstylists was not chosen.

Oh, Susanna is on the following page, using many of the above techniques and symbols.

OH, SUSANNA

Banjo: gDGBd

Stephen Foster
Arr.: P. W. Pardee

103

Appendix B

Music for Accompaniment
and
Alternate Notation Examples

Bass accompaniments for the Bach *Minuet* in the Intermediate section and the *Allegro* (BWV 998) from the Advanced section are given.

For the benefit of those accustomed to reading classic fingerstyle banjo music, *The Hussler Minor Jig* is presented again with the traditionally used annotation.

Next is the piano accompaniment for *Cupid's Arrow*. Classic fingerstyle banjo music often has piano parts.

A supplementary look at **Exercise A**, showing the essential source of all rolls is on page 114.

MINUET

J. S. Bach
Arr. - P. W. Pardee

From the Anna Magdalena Notebook

Bass, Banjo Minuet in G, concluded

ALLEGRO

From Prelude, Fugue and Allegro, BWV 998

Banjo: gDGBd

J. S. Bach
Arr. - Peter W. Pardee

Allegro, continued

Allegro, concluded

THE HUSSLER MINOR JIG

Banjo: gCGBd

Horace Weston

CUPID'S ARROW

Grand Polka de Concert.

Arranged by Vess L. Ossman

Cupid's Arrow, concluded

Another Look At Rolls

Banjo: gDGBd

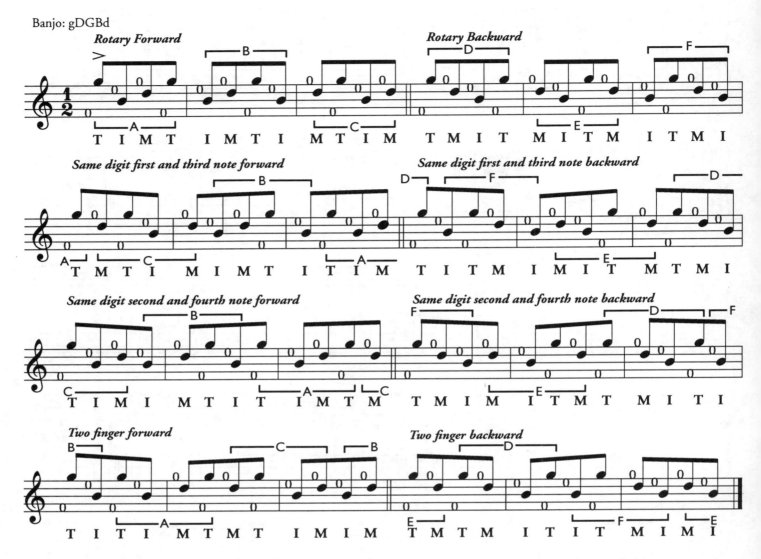

Viewed this way, all rolls come from forward and backward rolls, in reverse order and out of phase.

Appendix C

Projects to Do With Each Section

For the Beginner's Section

1. Page 13 - TUNING: Practice tuning your banjo over and over again. Tune down, rather than up, to put the banjo out of tune and you can avoid breaking strings.

2. Page 18 - TIMING and PITCH: Call out the names of the notes as you play them with a metronome. After you're playing in time with the metronome, play through exercises without the metronome. Then go back to playing with the metronome and compare your picking to the metronome to determine if you're playing steadily and consistently in time.

3. Page 20 - THE *G* MAJOR SCALE: Sing along with the first example as you play the notes, then with the second example, with the metronome at first, afterwards without the metronome. Then as in project 2, play with the metronome again, gradually increasing the *tempo*, or speed.

4. Page 21 - EXERCISE A: Because every four note combination of the three picking-hand fingers is given here, this exercise has many possibilities. Make up some ways to play this exercise that the author has not mentioned, such as different note values and accents. Re-order the measures, making sure the last note of any four note measure can link to the first note of any other measure with a different picking finger. All these will help you play with more freedom and agility. See page 114 for another way of looking at this exercise.

5. Pages 32-35 - JOHN HARDY I and II: Work out your own arrangement of John Hardy using the melody notes. Fill in some of the gaps in John Hardy I and II above the grid notes (diamond shaped note-heads). Don't be afraid to bring in the melody notes early or late—rolls can make this happen automatically, and the end result will be what's known as *syncopation*.

6. Work out a banjo arrangement of these two familiar public domain melodies on the next pages. Play the melody notes first (be careful to play them in time!) to find out what songs they are. Use the page, or photocopy the page, and write out your arrangement. First put the melody notes in place, then fill in roll notes from the chord, using pauses, or gaps, so that the music isn't too busy and so that the melody can come out strongly. Putting melody notes in places to more easily accomodate a roll is O.K., and will make for some syncopation. If it sounds good, fine, but if not, try changing things until you like the sound and can identify the melody coming out from all the helper notes. Don't stop with your first arrangement, but try them again. As your playing improves, your arrangements can, too.

For the Intermediate Section

1. Accents: Try arranging a tune with the accents described on page 22. The 1st and 4th, then the 3rd, and then the 2nd notes are accented with every set of four notes. See if a melody can be brought out accenting the notes as described above. Try the forward and backward rolls first, then try other rolls using the same accents.

2. More Songs: Arrange these songs, again using the grid as a guide to fill in notes, but this time be more attentive to leaving gaps where you think it 1) sounds better and 2) is easier to play. Refer to the accents and rhythms on pages 22 and 58 and use some of them.

3. Work more with the metronome and experiment with hand and arm positioning as shown on pages 37 and 38. Try for good tone, control of volume (loudness) and reduced pick noise (remember to use only a small amount of the finger and thumb picks digging into the strings—no more than 1/8 of an inch.)

Start at a slow metronome setting, and work up slowly, a notch at a time and learn to build up speed, all the while having exact control to play in time.

For the Advanced Section

1. Develop arrangements of the next songs. Choose a song you'd like to learn to play and make up your own arrangement from sheet music or tablature, or a recording.

2. Play through the 625 permutations with a metronome for 10 days in a row. Write in picking fingers for those sets that you get stuck on until you can play steadily without an interruption.

For the Extreme Section

1. Practice the three examples, *Swipesy Cakewalk*, the *Double* in c, and *Dominant Cycle Study #10* until you can play them up to or beyond the maximum recommended tempos on the music.

2. Choose music, either for solo banjo or with accompaniment that you would like to learn, and develop an arrangement.

3. Work on improvisation by singing lines from your imagination or listening experience, then try to play the lines on the banjo.

SONG I

Banjo: gDGBd

SONG II

Banjo - gDGBd

118

For the Intermediate Section

SONG III

Banjo: gDGBd

119

SONG IV

Banjo: gDGBd

For the Advanced Section
Banjo: gDGBd

SONG V

121

SONG VI

Banjo: gDGBd

Song VI, concluded

ENDORSEMENTS

It's all in the right hand—ask any fingerstyle banjoist (unless he's left handed!). Timing, tone, dynamics, syncopation—every element that gives string music its unique character and individuality—are brought to life by the picking fingers of the right hand. That's why Pete Pardee's book, *BANJO PICKING—A Complete Method*, is such an important addition to the body of instructional material available to banjo players today. It teaches students of all levels how to bring greater expression into their music through the use of various picking hand techniques.

Using a unique system of combined musical notation and traditional banjo tablature, Pardee takes banjo students through folk tunes like *Careless Love* and *Down in the Valley*, then moves on to more advanced pieces like Bill Keith's *Beating Around the Bush* and *Swipesy Cakewalk* by Scott Joplin and Arthur Marshall. Important picking techniques are discussed throughout which can help unlock the door to stylistic development.

The five string banjo is enjoying its greatest renaissance. *BANJO PICKING* provides an inspirational resource for all who love to play this exciting and ever-changing instrument.

—Bob Black

I have always been inspired by Pete Pardee's pioneering approach to the five-string banjo. He has a tremendous capacity for viewing the banjo objectively—free from preconceived stereotypes. Pete brings this spirit to bear in *BANJO PICKING*. This book presents Pete's methodical approach to unlocking the banjo's full potential as a musical instrument.

—John Bullard

BANJO PICKING will keep your interest regardless of your playing level, and is fun to work with. Designed with the right hand as the primary focus, this book offers far more than one could imagine. It will challenge both hands and expand your working knowledge of the fingerboard. Recommended for the beginning through the advanced level player.

—Janet Davis

Mr. Pardee has produced a wonderful book for the adventurous banio player.

—Wayne Erbsen

Whatever musical style you play on the five-string banjo—traditional bluegrass, fiddle tunes, single string jazz or something beyond to the instrument's outermost modern musical fringes—it's essential to have a good, solid right hand. In this volume, Pete Pardee has pushed forward the three-finger banjo envelope through a meticulously graded series of exercises which provide the necessary right hand foundation for great playing at any level and in any three-finger style. In addition, this volume will whip your left hand into shape, help you to understand some of the deepest mysteries of music theory as well as have you playing some choice tunes that range from J. S. Bach to ragtime-era classic banjo and even a jazz standard. All in all, this is a very deep and satisfying work that should provide years of enjoyment as a primary banjo reference.

—Bill Evans

Peter Pardee has written a carefully thought-out book for the student of the five-string banjo. He has covered everything so well from exacting notation to proper playing pedagogy that I don't see how anyone following this book can't become a good fingerstyle banjo player. *BANJO PICKING* serves as one of the best foundations for fingerstyle banjo playing ever written. It's a must for every bluegrass picker and classical banjo player as well.

—Frank Hamilton

For serious students of the five-string banjo, *BANJO PICKING* will provide a wealth of information and insight into the complexities of banjo picking. Whether you're a beginner or an advanced player, you'll find a lot to learn from Peter's well-organized and comprehensive course of study. Through many musical examples in a variety of styles including classical, ragtime, bluegrass, and jazz, Peter systematically explains all the picking-hand techniques essential to the complete banjoist—there's much within these pages to inspire both the budding musician and the seasoned professional. And his innovative conjoined notation, which bridges the gap between tablature and music notation, will help every banjoist to meet the challenges of new pieces of music and to discover and polish his or her own musical voice.

—Bill Keith

As a long time student of the five string banjo and its history, I am impressed with the wide range of information this book contains in only 128 pages. I'm especially pleased with the extensive use of both text and photos dealing with the proper right hand position and the use of finger picks. This is something usually glossed over in banjo methods. The use of the conjoined notation is a welcome addition as well, since this will help prepare the student for using non-banjo music in learning solos.

—Andy King

Pete has done the banjo community a great service with this exhaustive compendium of right hand patterns. Players at any level of experience will proft from a serious study of these roll exercises.

—John Lawless

There are many different choices for instructional material these days. Many more than when I started learning to play the banjo nearly 30 years ago. Now and then, a new choice will emerge that is clearly superior to its counterparts. Peter Pardee's book, *BANJO PICKING—A Complete Method*, is just such a choice. After going over the book myself and even incorporating it into my banjo instruction classes, it is easy to see that Peter's book offers players of all skill levels a wealth of banjo information. With his revolutionary idea of conjoined notation and his great attention paid to each little detail, Peter has developed a teaching resource that will be invaluable to aspiring banjoists everywhere.

If you are serious about learning to play the five string banjo or if you are someone who has hit the proverbial "wall" with your picking abilities, I highly recommend that you try *BANJO PICKING—A Complete Method*.

—Lynwood Lunsford

Peter Pardee, with the publication of *BANJO PICKING—A Complete Method*, has filled a gap long needed for the serious banjoist. It provides a learned look at the intricacies of the three finger approach used by players of the banjo from the classic to the bluegrass styles of playing. In great detail the author takes beginners and advanced player through the building blocks of the three finger approach to the five string banjo. Additionally, it offers a unique combination of tablature and standard musical notation—an excellent and painless way to learn to read music. This volume is not to be missed by the determined student of the instrument.

—Alan Munde

Peter Pardee's *BANJO PICKING* will make a wonderful addition to your banjo library. It's filled with tunes and exercises to sophisticate your right hand. You'll move from beginning to advanced (all comers are welcome in this inspiring tome) while dipping into the wellsprings of bluegrass, jazz, classical, and classic parlor styles. This will open your mind and ears and make you a more wide-ranging and versatile player. Well worth the price of admission.

—Tony Trischka

Pete Pardee has created a unique and inventive instructional product for banjo. With modern banjo styles demanding the widest possible range of note choices, Pete's exercises are structured to help a player become familiar with the range of possibilities. His system offers a formidable array of right hand patterns, helping the player to develop maximum flexibility and versatility.

—Pete Wernick

EXCELLENCE IN MUSIC

MEL BAY®

Since 1947